Flynn watche
as she slid into sleep

There was a funny ache in his chest. She looked so vulnerable. He set his glass down and stood up. He should probably wake her up and send her home. Ann wasn't going to be happy about falling asleep in front of him. It was too big a chink in the wall she kept between them. He looked at her a moment longer, then covered her with a blanket. Her hair was still pulled back in a loose bun, but a few strands had escaped the pins to curl around her face. He brushed them back, letting the soft warmth encircle his fingers.

He wasn't entirely sure what was happening between them, but he knew it was a lot more than just concern for Becky. Thirty-three was a hell of a time to fall in love for the first time. He'd almost begun to think it would never happen.

ABOUT THE AUTHOR

Dallas Schulze is a full-time writer who lives in Southern California with her husband and Persian cat. An avid reader, she devours romances by the boxful. In her spare time she enjoys doll collecting, doll making, sewing and watching old movies, especially Clark Gable films.

Books by Dallas Schulze

HARLEQUIN AMERICAN ROMANCE

154—MACKENZIE'S LADY
185—STORMWALKER

Tell Me a Story
Dallas Schulze

Harlequin Books

TORONTO • NEW YORK • LONDON
AMSTERDAM • PARIS • SYDNEY • HAMBURG
STOCKHOLM • ATHENS • TOKYO • MILAN

For Debra,
who could see the silk purse
lurking behind the sow's ear I handed her.
Thank you.

Published February 1988

First printing December 1987

ISBN 0-373-16235-9

Chapter One

The pile of newspapers was moving. Flynn peered at it carefully to make sure. Yes, it was definitely moving. This seemed odd when he thought about it. Everything else was rather foggy at the moment, but he was positive that newspapers did not move on their own.

Therefore, there must be something moving them. This piece of brilliant reasoning burst into his alcohol-soaked mind with the force of a lightning bolt. He nodded slowly, pleased with himself. And to think that he'd taken a cab because he thought he was too drunk to drive home. This proved how wrong he had been.

He slumped against the wall that held him upright and considered the problem. If the papers were not moving themselves, which he had decided was the case, he should know why they were moving. After all, this was his alley; he ought to know what was happening in it.

His eyes narrowed. *Was* it his alley? Now there was a point for him to bring up with the lawyers. Since the family owned the building, did that mean they owned the alley, too? That question ought to keep them busy for at least ten minutes. They might as well do something to earn the retainers they were paid.

The newspapers stirred again, drawing his wandering attention. He wet one long finger and held it up waveringly. Wind. That could be the cause. He was proud of this brilliant thought and rather irritated when he could feel no breeze on his damp finger.

When his gaze returned to the papers there was a definite frown drawing his black brows together. The papers shifted more violently this time and Flynn's frown deepened into a scowl. That was an arm. Thin and pale and amazingly fragile against the dark macadam, but still, it was definitely an arm.

Now he was going to have to investigate. No question about it. Whether it was technically his alley or not, he felt a proprietary interest in it. He couldn't just walk off and leave it in the possession of these animated and possibly dangerous papers.

Actually, he wasn't sure he could walk at all, he admitted with a flash of honesty. But that was neither here nor there. The point was—and he seemed to be having some difficulty in sticking to the point—it was his civic duty to find out exactly what was going on. What if this was the first wave of an invading force from another planet? This could be an alien pod looking for some innocent human to take over their body.

It didn't occur to Flynn that he was the only human within striking range of the potential pod, nor did he think that the alley behind a luxury apartment building in Los Angeles seemed an odd starting point for an interplanetary invasion. At five o'clock in the morning, after drinking all night, anything seemed not only possible but logical.

The ground showed a disconcerting tendency to tilt when he moved away from the wall but, filled with pixilated patriotism, Flynn managed to cross the space between himself and the suspicious papers. With some vague thought of protecting his back, he leaned against the concrete wall next to his target and slid bonelessly down it until he sat on the pavement.

His landing was not quite as clean as it could have been. The lump under his right thigh jerked alarmingly and the papers cascaded in all directions. This startling activity was accompanied by a muffled shriek of pain that settled into a high, childish voice.

"Hey! Get off my foot, you big ox." The foot in question was yanked out from under him.

Flynn found himself gazing into a small heart-shaped face, fine sandy brows drawn together in a fierce scowl. He smiled at the face in a friendly way. "Sorry about your foot."

The two studied each other in the gray predawn light that oozed between the high walls of the alley. Flynn's gaze was clear and alert. Only someone who knew him well would have seen the faint glaze that dulled the vivid blue of his eyes.

"Are you a pod?" His tone was interested, but not particularly concerned. "And if you're a pod, are you male or female, or doesn't it matter?"

The scowl on the little face returned in triplicate. "I'm not a pod. I'm a girl."

"Are you sure?" Flynn was vaguely disappointed. He'd been looking forward to telling his father that aliens had landed and they'd chosen McCallister property as their landing site. The old man would have had an apoplectic fit at their effrontery.

"Course I'm sure. There's no such thing as pods. That was only in a movie. If you're too drunk to know that you must be *really* drunk."

Flynn gave up the pleasing image of his father telling the aliens to get off his property and looked apologetic. "Plastered, I'm afraid. But then I didn't expect to be called on to decide matters of national importance. Are you sure you're not a pod?"

"Course I'm sure."

He sighed. "That's a relief. I'd really rather not have the fate of the world in my hands right now. If you're not a pod, what are you doing under that pile of papers?"

"I was trying to sleep," she told him with heavy sarcasm.

His brows rose. "Sleeping? Why were you sleeping under those papers? Wouldn't a bed be more comfortable?"

"Course it would, but I don't have a bed." The statement was flat, leavened with a touch of scorn.

Flynn's brows shot up until they almost met the heavy fall of black hair that drifted onto his forehead.

"No bed at all?" he asked. She shook her head and he echoed the gesture. "It doesn't seem fair. I have more beds than I know what to do with and you don't have one at all." He sat pondering the inequities of this for so long that the child leaned forward to see if he was still awake.

She jumped when he spoke suddenly. "Tell you what, you can use one of my beds. Help me up and we'll go to my 'partment and find you a bed. Bound to be a spare or two lying around the place."

He struggled to his feet, leaning one hand on his companion's shoulder once he achieved his goal. He frowned down at her. "You're not very big, are you?"

She drew herself up straighter, almost unbalancing him as she did so. "My mom says that being tall isn't important. Short people can move mountains, too."

He nodded, impressed by the profundity of this remark. "Very true. Come to think of it, I'm six-two and I've never moved a mountain. Just goes to prove that being tall isn't everything."

"Just a minute, mister." The piping voice interrupted his forward move, and he turned to look down at her, weaving slightly with checked momentum. "Are there any strings attached to this?"

He gave the question some consideration. "I don't think so. What kind of strings did you have in mind?"

She shook her head. "I don't know, but my mom always said that men don't make offers without strings."

"You know, the more I hear, the more I think your mother is a singularly intelligent woman."

She frowned a bit. "Well, I don't know about that, but she's real smart."

She guided his erratic footsteps across the alley and stopped in front of the door he indicated. He fumbled with the knob for a moment and then remembered it was locked. After a lengthy search for his keys, which turned up in the pocket of his gray slacks, his companion took the key ring from him and tried each key until she hit the right one.

The door closed behind them with an expansive whoosh of air. Flynn blinked rapidly in the sudden glare of light, though the short corridor was actually very softly lit. A bank of four elevators lined one wall.

With a great deal of concentration, he managed to punch out a short combination of numbers that opened the doors on the elevator. The two of them entered the thickly carpeted cubical and the doors swished shut. Flynn grabbed for the nearest wall as the floor surged upward, leaving his stomach somewhere beneath them.

"Are you okay, mister?" He closed his eyes in exquisite agony as the elevator stopped and the doors slid open, revealing a wide foyer and two beautifully carved wooden doors on either side.

A small hand tugged on his pant leg. "Are you gonna be sick, mister?"

He opened his eyes and looked down into her concerned little face. "I am never sick," he announced firmly, the words directed at least as much to his churning stomach as to the child.

Using her shoulder as a brace, he steered her out of the elevator and then stopped, trying to remember why he was here. A small voice recalled him to the task at hand.

"Which door, mister?"

Flynn turned slowly and then pointed to the door on the left, with a gesture worthy of Lady Macbeth. He shook his head with equal drama and then had to wait a moment for it to stop spinning.

"Don't go near that door. A dragon lives there."

"There's no such thing as dragons." The pragmatic statement did nothing to further the atmosphere Flynn had thought he was creating. He pulled his gaze from the door and looked down at his companion, his chin setting stubbornly.

"*I* live here and I happen to know that there is a dragon living there. We meet occasionally in the elevator. She has red hair and cold green eyes and she can freeze your bones with one look.''

''A dragon wouldn't fit in a elevator.''

''She's a very small dragon. Besides, I thought you said that there couldn't be a dragon because they didn't exist.''

His new acquaintance shook her head, her small face twisted in an expression of adult exasperation.

''You're drunker'n a skunk.''

Flynn frowned. ''We have already established that point. I see no reason to belabor it.''

He followed her lead to the other door and watched while she sorted through the key ring, trying each one in turn. He could have told her which key to use, but he was in no hurry. There was a pleasant buzzing sensation in his head. Sooner or later, the alcohol was going to catch up with him and he was going to regret the night's debauchery, but for now, he had no objections to standing outside his door.

The quiet snick of the lock interrupted his thoughts, and he reached out to push the door open. They stepped onto thick, soft carpeting and the door clicked quietly shut behind them. Flynn walked a few feet before realizing that something was wrong. He stopped and thought about it for a moment. He couldn't see anything. That was the problem. He spun on one heel with more enthusiasm than sense and stumbled against a narrow table. There was a faint thud as the table rattled beneath his weight and something fell to the floor.

His groping hands cleared the table of the remainder of its contents as he felt his way along the length of it, searching for the wall. He had just succeeded in finding it and was preparing to start the arduous task of locating the light switch when brilliant light suddenly flooded the hall.

He turned more slowly this time, then leaned back on the table and studied his companion. She stood on the opposite side of the hall, her hand just dropping away from the switch. He gave her a smile that had been known to make little old ladies swoon with pleasure.

She was not impressed. Her eyes took in the destruction he had left behind, and when she looked up at him her small mouth was pursed in stern disapproval.

"You're drunker than a skunk." It was obvious that his condition disgusted her, and Flynn tried his smile again, adding just a bit of coaxing apology to it. His new mentor only scowled deeper. "Look what a mess you made."

He cast his eyes on the scattered bric-a-brac that lay on the thick carpet, and shuddered. "Good grief. It looks like a miniature massacre." Small soldiers lay in positions suggestive of death and destruction. He gasped and clutched his chest theatrically. "Oh, my God! He shot me! The short guy in the gray suit shot me."

She giggled. "They're all short and there's lots of them in gray suits."

"Well, obviously, one of them recognized me as a Yankee through and through." He poked one of the little figures with an expensively shod foot. "My father's chess set. Trust him to have a chess set based on the Civil War." There was an old bitterness in the words.

He cocked his head, listening to the mellow chimes of the grandfather clock that stood in the living room.

"Six o'clock. The whole night is gone." He threw off the brief melancholy that had seized him and lurched away from the wall. "Come on. We've got to be in bed by six-thirty."

"How come?" The words were brought out on a yawn as she followed his unsteady path. He stumbled down the two steps that led into the living room and almost sprawled onto the carpet. Some rapid and surprisingly graceful footwork kept him upright, and he turned to grin at her triumphantly.

"Fred Astaire, eat your heart out," he exclaimed expansively.

She studied him critically. "Fred Astaire did things deliberately. *That* was an accident. Besides, you're not wearing a fancy black coat."

"How do you know he did things deliberately?" he asked mulishly. "I bet a lot of his best routines were accidents. And what's wrong with my clothes?"

He tilted his head to look down at himself. Gray slacks and a blue silk shirt that matched his eyes were topped by a suede jacket. He had thought the outfit looked fine when he'd put it on earlier in the evening.

His companion ignored his question and returned to a more important issue. "How come we've got to be in bed by six-thirty?"

He blinked at her as if trying to remember where he was and then gave a sudden gasp. "Six-thirty. Oh, my God! We've got to hurry." He reached out to grab her shoulder and steered a weaving path across the living room. He stopped in the hall and gave her an intent look, bending down to look her in the eye.

"If I'm still up at six-thirty, I turn into a vampire."

Her eyes widened. "Really?"

He nodded solemnly and straightened up, grabbing onto a convenient doorjamb when his head spun. "It's an old family curse," he said sadly. "Every morning at six-thirty, we all turn into vampires."

She eyed him suspiciously. "Everybody knows that people turn into vampires at night and if they're caught out in the *sun*, they die."

"They do?" He seemed impressed with this information. "Do you mean to tell me I've been doing it wrong all these years?" He shook his head. "I might have known I'd screw it up."

She caught the twinkle in his eye and giggled. "You're very silly." The words were obviously a compliment, and Flynn accepted them in the spirit intended.

"Thank you. I do my best." He stood away from the wall, swaying for a moment before regaining his balance. His lips twisted in a rueful smile. "I'm afraid my night of wicked carousing is catching up with me." He blinked to clear his foggy vision. "We'd better get you settled before I collapse."

He set his feet down with neat precision, each step carefully planned and executed as he led the way through one of the doors that faced onto the hallway. The bedroom was beautifully done in shades of brown and slate blue. Plush blue carpeting and drapes formed a background for the rich mahogany furniture.

He stopped in the doorway and swept one hand out in invitation. Slowly, the little girl moved into the room, staring around her with wide gray eyes.

"Wow."

The soft exclamation drew Flynn's wandering gaze back to her. The pain that had darkened his vivid eyes softened and disappeared as he took in the wondering little face. In her childish eyes, the room was reflected as a palace and, for an instant, he saw her vision, pushing aside the hurtful memories that tainted it.

"Not bad, huh?"

"Wow." That one word expressed absolute awe. She tiptoed across the thick carpet and reached out to touch the heavy bedspread, drawing back before her hand made contact. The gesture spoke volumes. A stab of anger cleared Flynn's foggy mind for a moment, and he crossed the room in a few quick strides and grabbed hold of the bedspread, jerking it off the bed and tossing it carelessly on the floor.

She gasped as if he had committed a sacrilege, but he ignored her, pulling down the crisp linen sheets to poke a careless hand into the already fluffed pillows. When he turned to look at her, she was staring at him wide-eyed, sensing a difference that even he didn't quite understand.

He sat on the foot of the bed and smiled at her. "They're only things," he said softly.

"But it's so beautiful." She bent to touch the discarded bedspread reverently. His eyes followed her hand and, for a moment, he could almost imagine that he heard laughter and saw Mark winking at him, his eyes almost the same color as the spread. He blinked and the moment was gone.

"It's beautiful, but it's only a thing. It's all right to admire things but don't ever become obsessed with them." Silence filled the beautiful room for a minute as he looked around, seeing everything the same as it had been all those years ago. "Maybe it's time to make some changes," he murmured softly.

He shook his head and got to his feet, looking down at his diminutive companion. "Make yourself at home. This is a good room. It used to belong to my brother, but he doesn't need it anymore. Still, the room must remember him," he said whimsically.

She watched him silently, only speaking when he would have pulled the door shut behind him. "Hey, mister, could you leave the door open?"

He stuck his head around the door and grinned at her. "You bet, and I'll leave the hall light on, too. My bedroom is two doors down on the right. If you need anything, just come in and poke me. Good night, urchin."

Flynn walked the few feet to his bedroom, deliberately encouraging the alcoholic fumes to cushion his mind. Once in the room, he collapsed on the wide bed, oblivious to the richly masculine surroundings. He shrugged out of his jacket and tossed it in the general direction of a chair and then tugged off his shoes, letting them fall where they would.

He leaned back on the thick pile of pillows and put his hands behind his head, staring up at the ceiling and seeing his brother's face mirrored there. The features marked them as brothers but the coloring set them apart. Mark had inherited their father's reddish-brown hair and dark eyes, and Flynn was a throwback to his mother's grandfather. With his black hair and bright blue eyes he was altogether too flamboyant to be a staid McCallister. Mark's imagined eyes crinkled with amusement, and Flynn could hear his brother telling him that self-pity never did anyone any good. He blinked and the image was gone.

He groaned softly. God, he was drunk. He hadn't been this badly smashed in years. Not since he and

Mark... No. He didn't want to remember that. Not now. Not when his defenses were at an all-time low.

The memories faded and were replaced by tiny features capped with a mop of raggedly cut sandy hair. His mouth tilted up. Cute little thing. Who was she? Good Lord, he didn't even know her name! Oh well, in the morning he could find out her name and find her parents and get her back where she belonged.

The mists of drink and exhaustion gradually thickened, creating swirling pockets of peace in his tired thoughts. The faint lines beside his mouth smoothed out as his breathing deepened and slowed, his long body relaxing into the cozy comfort of the bedspread.

He stirred once a few minutes later, some half-buried sense telling him that something was different. But he didn't wake even when the door closed quietly behind a tiny figure.

She froze just inside the door as the man on the bed stirred, and then breathed a silent sigh of relief when he relaxed again. Small bare feet moved quietly across the plush carpet until she stood at the edge of the bed. Moving ever so slowly and quietly, she turned back the corner of the bedspread and eased onto the bed.

The other room was pretty, but it was awfully big and lonely and, for the moment, this strange man offered safety in an unknown world.

She curled up against the pillow, one thin arm encircling a battered toy giraffe, the other hand tucked up under her cheek.

By the time the grandfather clock struck seven, man and child were fast asleep, the arms of Morpheus holding them both safe and secure.

Chapter Two

Flynn's nose twitched and his eyelids flickered. A muffled groan was smothered in the pillow as he buried his face deeper in the soft down. If the pillow were just a little bigger, he could find a way to sink his whole body into it and pull it shut behind him.

He was dying. That was the only possible excuse for this much pain.

His head hurt with a relentless, pounding throb that moved from the top of his skull all the way down his body. Even his toes ached. It was unfortunate that amnesia didn't go along with the ache. Then he wouldn't have been able to remember drinking himself into a stupor. At least he'd had the sense to take a taxi home.

He was getting too old for this kind of nonsense. At thirty-three he ought to know better than to try and lose himself in a bottle. It didn't make the memories go away and it didn't bring back the dead. Well, Mark's birthday had come and gone. Another year past and he still hadn't managed to put his brother's death behind him. But then, maybe that kind of thing was never really behind you.

His head hurt too much for philosophical questions. Right now he wasn't sure he could deal with the present problems, let alone the past. Present problems... There was something nagging at the back of his mind. Something he should remember about the previous night.

He frowned and then wished he hadn't. Changing expressions only made the pain worse. He could remember paying the taxi off, and then he'd wandered into the alley and there'd been something there.... The newspapers—and the little girl.

He gathered what little strength remained in his body and rolled onto his back. For the moment, he didn't try to open his eyes. His nose twitched again. What was that smell? Acrid and smoky. Was the apartment on fire? The thought forced his eyes open. No sign of smoke. The soft light hurt his eyes and he had to narrow his eyelids. He sniffed again. What was that smell?

"Are you awake, mister?" He rolled onto his side toward the voice. The little girl from the night before was perched on the edge of a chair she'd pulled next to the bed.

"I'm awake but I'm not sure I'm alive." His voice came out in a scratchy growl, which pretty much described how he felt.

"I made you some coffee. Mom always wants coffee when she has a hangover."

"Bless you." He dragged himself into a sitting position, propping his back against the headboard. His clothes seemed to crackle when he moved or maybe that was his bones. He really was getting too old for all-night binges.

The child got up, lifted a cup off the night table and handed it to him, holding it carefully with both hands. Flynn took it from her the same way, hoping the tremor in his right hand would counteract the quiver in his left.

He lifted the cup to his mouth and took a sip. If the synapses in his brain hadn't been so saturated with alcohol, they would have had time to warn him. As it was, by the time the message had gotten from his nose to his hands that the acrid smell was coming from the cup he held, he'd already taken a hearty mouthful of the liquid inside.

As a method of waking someone up, the brew was probably unequaled. Flynn's eyes sprang from half-mast to wide open. He sat up straighter in bed and, for an instant, he forgot about his headache.

The substance in his mouth might have been a primeval predecessor to coffee, but it bore only a vague resemblance to the smooth brew usually associated with the word. The acrid, smoky scent that had led him to wonder if the apartment was on fire was amplified in the taste. The liquid was thick, slightly rancid in flavor and so strong that it threatened to dissolve the enamel on his teeth.

He was about to spit the foul liquid back into the cup when his eyes fell on his small houseguest. Wide gray eyes peered from beneath ragged, sandy bangs. Their expression reminded him of a puppy who'd just performed a difficult trick and was hoping for a reward. Without another thought, he swallowed the liquid, praying that his stomach lining was tougher than it felt. He smiled, wondering if his teeth had actually been etched by their contact with the alleged coffee.

"It's wonderful."

His companion smiled. The beaming expression changed her from waiflike to almost angelic. Just for that look, it was worth the suspicion that his stomach would never be the same.

"Mom says you can't start a day without coffee."

"I . . . ah . . . feel the same way." Flynn tried to look casual as he held the cup in his lap, as far from his nose as possible. Would the stuff eat through the porcelain? "Could you get me a damp washcloth, do you think? The bathroom is through there."

"Sure." She hopped off her chair and trotted away. Flynn looked frantically for a place to dispose of the cup's contents. He didn't dare drink the stuff. He might survive a swallow, but a full cup would certainly be fatal. Water was running in the bathroom. He had only a moment. A quick tilt of his wrist dumped the liquid into the base of the philodendron that sat under a plant light next to the bed.

Was it his imagination, or did the plant shudder with the impact of the brew?

His guest came back into the bedroom carrying a dripping cloth, and Flynn set the empty cup down, trying to look as if he'd drained it and felt much better for the experience. He held out his hand, trying not to grimace at the icy cold, sopping wet cloth that landed in his palm. With an apology to the innocent philodendron, he wrung the cloth out in the pot before wiping his face with it.

The cold cloth didn't help much. His head still pounded and his eyes were still gritty. But his miseries were going to have to wait.

"I don't think we were properly introduced last night. I'm Flynn McCallister."

"I'm Rebecca Antoinette Sinclair."

Flynn's brows arched, meeting the black hair that fell onto his forehead. "Good grief. That's a mouthful. Do I have to use the whole thing every time?" He looked so appalled that she giggled.

"You can call me Becky." She picked up the empty cup and peered into it. Flynn wouldn't have been surprised to see that the bottom had been eaten away. "Do you want some more coffee?"

"No! I mean, it was delicious but one cup is my limit." He hoped his smile wasn't as sickly as it felt. The pounding in his head had returned a hundredfold. All he wanted to do was roll over in bed and die. Barring that, he was willing to try a long, steaming hot shower. He looked at Becky and knew that both plans were out of the question.

"I was not quite myself last night...."

"You were drunker than a waltzin' pissant." She said it so firmly that Flynn gave up any thought of arguing his condition.

"All right. I was drunk." He caught her eye and amended the statement. "Very drunk. But that's neither here nor there." He hurried on before she could argue the point. "I seem to recall that you were sleeping in the alley. Now, it's been a while since I was your age, but I'm sure I'd remember if sleeping in alleys was normal. Where's your mom and dad?"

"I don't have a daddy." Her chin thrust out, defying him to say anything. "He left when I was real little, but Mom and me don't need him. We do just fine on our own."

"Okay. What about your mom? Where is she? She must be worried sick about you."

The tough little chin quivered. "I don't know. She was s'posed to come home a couple weeks ago. Only she didn't."

Flynn swung his legs over the side of the bed and sat up. He wished his head would quit hurting. "Where did she go?"

"She went away with one of her boyfriends. She's real pretty and she has lots of boyfriends. She was supposed to come back on Monday. Only she didn't."

"Don't you think you should have stayed at home, so she'd know where to find you?"

"I did for a while. But then Mrs. Castle said she was going to report me to the welfare people 'cause I'd been left. But Mama didn't leave, and if the welfare people take me away, I'll never see her again. Mama told me all about them. And I'm scared that somethin' may have happened to her. Only Mrs. Castle wouldn't listen to me. She told me I was just a kid and I didn't know nothin'. But I know Mama wouldn't leave me."

"Who is Mrs. Castle?"

It took a while and some judicious questioning but eventually Flynn pieced together what he thought was a fairly accurate picture. Apparently, Becky's mother frequently left Becky on her own for the weekend while she went off with one of her many boyfriends. This was an established pattern, and Becky saw nothing wrong with it. She was very good at taking care of herself, she informed him.

Two weeks ago her mother had left as usual. To Becky, the boyfriend was just a faceless man named John. This, too, was normal. Becky never met her mother's escorts, which made Flynn wonder just what kind of boyfriends her mother had. This time her mother hadn't come back from the weekend trip.

Mrs. Castle managed the apartment building where Becky and her mother lived. She'd become alarmed by the mother's continued absence. Flynn couldn't help but wonder if her alarm hadn't been sparked by the fact that the rent had come due. She told Becky she was going to call the welfare department, and Becky packed a paper bag with her most important belongings and ran away. The welfare people and the bogeyman were apparently much the same in Becky's young mind. She'd been living on the streets for the past three days, and Flynn shuddered to think of what could have happened to her.

"You know, you can't just disappear like that, Becky. What's going to happen when your mom goes home and you aren't there? She's going to be worried."

Becky's brows came together. "I know. But I couldn't let the welfare people take me away. They'd never let me see her again."

Flynn rubbed a hand over the stubble on his chin. He felt unwashed, unkempt and unfit to handle this problem. He closed his eyes, half hoping Becky would turn out to be a figment of an alcohol-soaked imagination. But when he opened them again, she was still sitting there, her eyes fixed on him.

He sighed.

"You won't call the welfare people, will you, Mr. Flynn?"

He looked at her, wondering what imp of fate had chosen to drop her into his lap. Was fate testing him or her? Of the two of them, she was probably getting the worse bargain.

"It's just Flynn. And, no, I won't call the welfare people."

"What are you going to do with me?" She looked at him with absolute trust, clearly depending on him to make the best decision about her future. Flynn wanted to scream. Instead, he thrust his fingers through his hair and stood.

"The first thing I'm going to do is clean up and then we'll consider our options before we make any rash decisions."

"Does that mean I can stay here for a while?"

"That means you can stay here for a while."

"Do you think I could have something to eat?"

Flynn was almost to the bathroom door and the nirvana of a hot shower when the question reached him. He stopped and turned to look at his small guest. She was so independent and self-sufficient that it was hard to remember she was only a child. He swallowed a surge of self-directed anger.

"Didn't you get something while you were making coffee?"

"I wasn't sure if it would be okay. Mom says you should always wait to be invited."

"Consider this a permanent invitation. My home is open to you, madam. Feel free to avail yourself of all its facilities." He bowed low, and the sound of her giggle almost made him forget that his head was threatening to fall off his shoulders.

"Let's go see what the cupboard holds."

Luckily for the state of his stomach, Becky opted for cold cereal. Unfortunately, the remains of her coffee-brewing venture still sat in a pan on the stove. Flynn approached it cautiously, half expecting a scaled monster to rise up over the rim of the pot. Surely, the primordial goo from which life sprang must have smelled something like this.

Nothing lunged at him and, once he got a look in the pot, he could see why. No life form could possibly survive in the sullen black murk in the pot. He thought of the philodendron and winced. Not even a plant deserved a death like that.

"How did you make the coffee, Becky?" He grasped the handle of the pot with two fingers and inched it off the burner in the direction of the sink.

Becky looked up from her cereal. "Well, I couldn't find the regular stuff. But there was this jar in your 'frigerator and it said coffee. I can read," she interjected, clearly proud of this fact. Flynn made an appropriate noise and tilted the pot's contents into the sink, half expecting the stainless steel to melt on contact.

"Anyway, it didn't look like coffee but it said coffee so I tried to make some like I always make Mom. I boiled some water real careful 'cause Mom says you always got to be careful with stoves. And then I put some of that stuff in a cup. It was all in big lumps instead of powdery like real coffee. I tried to mash it with a spoon but it didn't work so I poured the water over it. I thought maybe the lumps would melt. Only they didn't and it didn't look right so I dumped it all back in the pan and boiled it for a long time. Those lumps never did go away but it turned the right color. You really ought to buy some new coffee, Mr. Flynn. I think that stuff's gotten old."

Flynn thought of the twenty-five-dollar-a-pound Jamaican Blue Mountain coffee beans that she'd massacred. The laugh started deep in his belly and worked its way out. Becky looked up from her food as

Flynn leaned against the counter and gave in to the laughter, clutching at his pounding head. She looked at him for a moment and then shrugged.

It was several minutes before Flynn regained control. "I'm going to pick up the paper and the mail and then I'm going to take a hot shower. Then we'll sit down and talk about what we're going to do with you." She nodded, more interested in trying to find a way through the maze on the back of the cereal box.

Flynn left her to the puzzle and went to the front door. His mouth was still curved in a smile. Sometimes it took a child to put things into clear perspective. He unbuttoned his shirt. As soon as he picked up the paper, he was going to spend at least an hour under steaming hot water.

He stepped into the hall just as the elevator slid to a halt. Since he wasn't expecting any visitors, there was only one person it could be—his neighbor. His smile took on a wicked edge.

Ann Perry had lived in the apartment across from him for two years. She was young, attractive, single, and she sternly disapproved of him. She made that clear every time their paths happened to cross. She was a doctor at a local hospital, and the fact that he was sometimes arriving home just as she was going to work obviously offended her sensibilities.

It was unkind, but he could never quite resist the urge to reinforce her image of him as a worthless, womanizing playboy. When those green eyes looked at him as if expecting him to sprout horns and a tail, it brought out a particularly wicked streak. He stopped short of throwing an orgy just to confirm her opinions, but he doubted that she needed any additional proof of his worthlessness.

He turned toward the elevator and leaned one shoulder against the doorjamb. He knew exactly the picture he presented. It was four o'clock in the afternoon. He was unshaven. His hair was tousled. His feet were bare. His shirt was unbuttoned to the waist and his belt was unbuckled. He looked the very picture of worthless masculinity. It was perfect.

The elevator doors slid open, and Flynn felt a twinge of guilt. In the instant before she saw him, she looked tired. There was a vulnerable droop to her shoulders that made him want to offer her a place to rest her head. But it was only a momentary illusion. The moment her eyes fell on him, her shoulders stiffened into a military stance and her eyes turned a frosty shade of green.

Flynn slumped against the wall, letting his eyes trail insolently over her, from the tips of her neat black pumps—the heels a sensible two inches—over the gray suit—still crisp after a day spent at the hospital—to fine-boned features set in rigid disapproval and finally stopped on fiery red hair pulled into a smooth chignon.

When she'd first moved in, he'd had more than one fantasy about seeing that hair spread across his pillow, but it hadn't taken long for the message to come across that the fire in her hair didn't melt the ice in her eyes.

"Ms. Perry. Home from a day of saving lives?"

She tilted her head, her shoulders absolutely rigid as she stepped out of the elevator. "Mr. McCallister. Home from a night of drinking?"

She stalked to her door, stopping to pick up her mail and the newspaper. Flynn admired the line of her back. She really was a very attractive woman. If she'd just show some signs of humanity, he'd be able to resist the urge to live down to her opinion of him. He allowed himself a mental sigh of regret as she opened her door. Oh well, a dedicated doctor probably wasn't his style, anyway.

Right now the only female he had to worry about was about three feet tall and made a deadly cup of coffee.

Ann was aware of Flynn McCallister's eyes following her every move. Hands that were solid as a rock holding a needle suddenly felt remarkably quivery gathering up her mail. He didn't say anything more, but he didn't have to. Just his presence was enough to unnerve her.

She fumbled with the key before getting it in the lock. The door opened and she stepped into the haven of her home. She resisted the urge to slam the door. She wouldn't give him the satisfaction of knowing he disturbed her. The door closed with a quiet snick, enclosing her in the safety of her apartment and shutting him out.

"Ridiculous. You're acting like a child." Only there was nothing childlike about the feelings Flynn McCallister stirred.

The muttered reprimand didn't make her feel any less relieved, but it did bring her housemate running. She saw him coming across the living room and quickly dropped her mail and the paper on the hall table, emptying her arms. She was just in time. Three feet away, he launched himself into the air. Ann braced herself against the impact as seventeen pounds of gray fur landed in her arms.

It was Oscar's preferred method of greeting. It had been cute when he was a kitten. If he got any bigger, it was going to become life threatening, but Ann didn't have the heart to discourage him. It was nice to have someone excited about seeing her at the end of the day.

She carried the huge tomcat into the kitchen and set him on the floor. He jumped up on a stool and sat down to watch her make a snack. It was a ritual they carried out every afternoon. Oscar never begged for scraps, but if Ann happened to be fixing something he particularly liked, he was not above an occasional moan of hunger. He was judicious in his use of this technique. But roast beef was well worth the effort.

"Moocher." Ann chose a pink slice of beef and cut it into Oscar-size bites. He waited politely until she'd set the saucer on the floor before launching himself toward the treat. The meat was gone before Ann had finished making her sandwich, and Oscar returned to his stool to keep her company while she ate.

She set the plate down and then poured herself a glass of milk. Before she sat down to enjoy her snack, she slipped off her jacket and unbuttoned the first three buttons of her blouse. Her shoes had been abandoned on the way to the kitchen. She sat down but didn't reach for the sandwich. For just a moment she savored the stillness of the apartment. It wasn't that the hospital was noisy, but it was filled with such self-conscious quiet that there were times when she would have welcomed some healthy noise.

"I saw McCallister in the hall. He looked like he'd been up all night. Again. It's a good thing he doesn't try to hold down a job. It might interfere with his love life."

Oscar looked up from the paw he was washing and murmured sympathetically. He was familiar with the problem of McCallister. Ann smiled at the cat and took a healthy bite of her sandwich. Oscar was a great audience. He always agreed with her.

She chewed slowly, her eyes focused on nothing in particular. What was it about Flynn McCallister that never failed to irritate her? When she'd first moved in, she'd been prepared to be a cordial neighbor. Her father had pointed out that the McCallister family was wealthy and old power. Ann wasn't terribly interested in her neighbor's antecedents as long as he was quiet and didn't expect to borrow a cup of sugar at two-thirty in the morning.

At least that's what she thought before she'd met Flynn McCallister. He seemed to fit her simple criteria for neighborly behavior. He didn't throw wild parties. He was always polite. He'd never asked to borrow a cup of sugar at any time of day or night. In fact, they didn't run into each other very often. Sometimes it was a week or more between sightings.

Considering how little she saw of him, he took up an inordinate amount of room in her thoughts. Most of it hostile. It was the way he looked at her. Every time they met, those electric blue eyes seemed to strip her naked. And it wasn't just her clothes he was seeing through. It was as if he could see right through to her soul. Not that she had anything to hide, Ann told herself. It was just that she didn't like feeling naked in front of a total stranger.

And it didn't help at all to know that it was deliberate. He knew exactly what he was doing. He enjoyed flustering her. It annoyed Ann that he could read her so easily, and it annoyed her even more that she couldn't control her reaction to him. She was a doctor. People's lives rested in her hands every day. Control was essential in her work, and it carried over into her private life. With nothing but a look and a quirk of an eyebrow, Flynn McCallister managed to weaken that control, and she resented it.

It was resentment that made her feel so flushed and breathless when he looked at her. It was simple curiosity that made her wonder what it would feel like when he kissed someone. Not her, of course. She had no desire to kiss a man who couldn't even hold a job. It was just that he'd probably kissed a lot of women and she'd never been kissed by an expert. It was natural that she was curious.

"But we know where curiosity gets you, don't we, Oscar? Look what happened to the cat." Oscar blinked at her and then hopped down off the stool and trotted into the living room. "Oh dear. Maybe I shouldn't have mentioned it."

His tail disappeared around the corner with an indignant flip and Ann giggled. It was a girlish sound that would have surprised a lot of people who thought they knew her. Her colleagues at work had never heard Dr. Perry giggle. It was rare for her to bestow so much as a smile on anyone but a patient.

Despite the fiery warmth of her hair, she had a reputation for being icy cold. She did her work with a slightly feverish dedication that earned her respect, but she kept too much distance between herself and her colleagues to earn anything more than respect.

When Ann took time to think about it, she told herself she preferred it that way. She didn't really have time for all the foolish machinations that seemed to go along with friendships. Her work was too important to her. It filled her life quite nicely. If there were times when she saw two nurses laughing together and felt a little wistful, it was only when she was tired.

The phone rang, startling her out of her thoughts, and she jumped. It rang again, but she didn't move immediately. It would be her father. He would want a progress report. How did she tell him that a medical career wasn't like being a corporate executive where every day she could report some deal closed, some new advance toward a vice presidency? The triumphs of helping a patient didn't interest him in the least. He wanted to know where her career was going. He thought she was progressing too slowly.

The phone rang again, and she got to her feet. If she didn't answer it now, he would only call again later. Besides, it was wonderful that he was so interested in her career. It showed that he loved her.

Twenty minutes later she put down the phone, feeling more drained than when she'd left the hospital. Why couldn't she make him understand that medicine was usually a day-to-day grind with occasional advances? You didn't start out as a medical student and work your way to head of staff in ten days or less. Why couldn't he be proud of what she *had* accomplished instead of demanding to know why she hadn't done more? She suppressed the question before it had a chance to take root. He *was* proud of her. He just didn't know how to show it. He wasn't a demonstrative man, that's all.

She wandered back to the kitchen table and picked up her half-eaten sandwich. The food didn't look as good as it had a few minutes ago. She wrapped the sandwich in plastic wrap and rinsed out her milk glass. She was just tired. That's why her father's call was upsetting. That's why Flynn McCallister had seemed particularly dangerous.

She'd planned to go out and do some shopping, but maybe it would be a good idea to take a long hot bath and spend the evening with a book. She could use the time to unwind. She had the next two days off, and a relaxing evening at home would be a nice way to start her small vacation.

She left the kitchen and headed toward her bedroom, but she was sidetracked by Oscar who was sprawled flat on his back in the middle of the living-room floor. She stopped to scratch his ample tummy, and he took it as an invitation to play, wrapping his paws around her arm and chewing on her hand. His teeth sank gently into her fingers, careful not to bite too hard, and Ann responded by twisting her hand back and forth.

The sudden pounding on the door interrupted the playful wrestling match. Ann jumped, jerking her hand away from the cat so suddenly that she inflicted a scratch on her arm when his claws sprang out in automatic reaction to the sudden noise. Oscar rolled to his feet and streaked for the safety of the bedroom.

Ann stood up, staring at the door warily. No one had rung up from the lobby. Her father had just called her from the other side of town, and he was the only person she'd given the elevator code to. Of course, there was no telling how many people McCallister had handed out the code to. Maybe it was a friend of his who was too drunk to realize he had the wrong door.

The pounding started again. She would direct whoever it was to the correct apartment and then she'd make it a point to complain to the management company. McCallister couldn't just go around giving out security codes.

She grasped the doorknob, full of righteous indignation. This time he'd gone too far. It was one thing for him to be out at all hours of the day and night, and it was none of her business how many bimbos he brought home with him, but this was a matter of her own personal safety. She couldn't have him giving privileged information to all and sundry.

She yanked the door open, ready to give whoever it was her iciest look—the one that had been known to cow junior nurses at a glance. She'd make it clear that she didn't approve of his intrusion on her time. Her lips parted to deliver a scathing put-down, but not a word emerged. Instead of the inebriated sot she'd expected to see, she was nose to nose with a masculine chest. Broad, muscled and matted with hair. She knew it was matted with hair because it was bared to her gaze. In fact, there was not a stitch of clothing in sight. Her eyes dropped automatically to find that the only apparel her visitor was wearing was a towel—a rather small one—knotted carelessly around his hips. Her eyes jerked upward, and she took an automatic step backward.

The last thing she'd expected to find on her doorstep was Flynn McCallister, clad in nothing but a towel and a panicked expression.

Chapter Three

She was so disconcerted by this unexpected apparition that it took her several seconds to make any sense out of his words. Despite her best efforts, her eyes kept falling to his chest. There was something about that expanse of masculine skin that put a catch in her breathing and made her feel flushed.

She blinked, forcing her mind to function again. He was saying something. She dragged her eyes from his chest and looked at his face. Something was wrong. What was he saying?

"...in the shower and she fell. There's blood all over. I don't think a Band-Aid is going to do it. Maybe she needs stitches. You've got to come and take a look at her."

The doctor in her took over at the mention of blood. "I'll be right there. Keep her quiet and apply firm pressure to the wound. I'll get my bag."

Flynn disappeared in a flurry of blue towel and Ann hurried back into the living room. She grabbed up her bag, her mind working a mile a minute. The doctor in her was speculating on what the medical situation might be, wondering if it would be necessary to call for an ambulance. The woman, shoved well to the back, was speculating on other things, like whether or not her neighbor lifted weights. That would explain those sleek muscles that had rolled so easily under his skin.

In the shower and she fell. Flynn's half-heard explanation popped into her head, and her lips tightened in disapproval. Obviously, he had been cavorting in the shower with a woman, and she'd fallen. Probably hit her head, which would explain all the blood. There was a small, nasty part of Ann that muttered that she probably deserved it.

None of these frantic thoughts slowed her pace as she hurried out of her apartment and across the carpeted hall. She entered his apartment through the open door. She didn't have to look far for her patient. Flynn was kneeling on the floor next to one of the sofas, his naked back blocking Ann's view.

"She's a doctor and she'll know just what to do." His voice was soothing and full of confidence. A good bedside manner, she noted absently.

"But you said that a dragon lived next door." The voice was definitely feminine and just as definitely under ten years of age.

Ann tripped on the steps that had almost been Flynn's downfall the night before. Her recovery was not as graceful as his had been, but she didn't have the advantage of eight hours of steady drinking under her belt.

Flynn glanced over his shoulder, his face expressing his relief at her presence in the moment before he turned back to his companion. "I was kidding about that. She's really very nice." He didn't sound in the least embarrassed at having it revealed that he'd called her a dragon. Ann filed the words away to examine at some other time. Right now, what mattered was her patient.

Stepping around Flynn, she knelt by the sofa. Other than being female, the child bore no resemblance to her hasty image of a woman who'd been cavorting in Flynn's shower. She was small-boned and fragile with a mop of badly cut sandy hair that was matted with blood on one side. Her gray eyes were swimming with tears and an occasional sob shook her thin frame. She examined Ann solemnly without releasing her hold on Flynn's left hand. His right hand held a kitchen towel to the side of her head.

The scenario was not quite what Ann had been expecting, but the injury was exactly what she'd expected. Head wounds were always frightening, but they had a tendency to bleed out of all proportion to their seriousness.

"Becky, this is Ann. She's going to take care of your head for you."

Ann smiled at the little girl, unaware of the way her face lit and softened with the smile. "Hi, Becky. It looks like you smacked your head pretty good." She eased the towel away and was relieved to see that the actual wound itself was not too bad. A small cut at the end of Becky's eyebrow still oozed blood sullenly, but it wasn't enough to warrant stitches.

"Are you going to stick a needle in me?" Becky's lip quivered at the thought.

"I don't think we need to do that. A bandage should take care of this."

"I was in the shower and I heard her fall. I don't know what happened. She was looking at magazines when I went into the bathroom." Flynn's voice was tight with concern.

"I was just trying to get a closer look at that picture on the wall, Mr. Flynn. I stood up on the sofa, but I slipped on a book and hit my head on the table." Ann glanced over her shoulder at the coffee table. It was a massive affair of glass and wood. Becky was probably lucky the damage was as minor as it was.

"Is she going to be all right?" Flynn hadn't moved from his position beside Becky, but he managed to give off an aura of hovering that made Ann want to swat him like an obnoxious fly.

"She's going to be fine. Why don't you go boil some water?"

He seemed relieved to have something to do, and he hurried off to the kitchen. Ann watched him leave, trying to convince herself that he looked ridiculous in the barely decent towel. It didn't work. In fact, he looked distressingly sexy. She dragged her mind and her eyes back to her small patient.

Becky's eyes met hers solemnly, more than a trace of uncertainty in their depths. Ann smiled and the look faded a bit, but it wasn't replaced by trust. Ann had a feeling that this was not a child who trusted easily.

"What's the water for?"

"Nothing. He was making me nervous."

The little girl's eyes widened. "You mean you don't really need any water?"

"Nope. I don't need it at all. Men aren't very good at coping with things like this. They get all upset. I thought it would be a good idea if we got him out of our hair."

"Won't Mr. Flynn be mad?"

"I don't think so." Ann set the bloodstained towel on the glass-topped coffee table. Becky winced when

Ann tried to cleanse the wound, and Ann gave her a reassuring smile. "This may sting a little bit, but it won't hurt much, I promise."

"Mama always says that but it hurts a lot."

"Well, maybe your mother doesn't have the right stuff so it hurts more than she thinks it will. But I'm a doctor and this is a special cleanser that doesn't hurt a lot. Okay?"

The gray eyes studied Ann for a long moment, weighing and considering in a very adult manner. Ann didn't try to rush the decision, letting Becky take her time. It was much easier to work with children if they felt they had some control over what was happening to them. Becky finally nodded, apparently making up her mind that she'd trust Ann this time.

She dabbed the cotton against the cut, feeling the tension in Becky's frame. "Is Flynn a friend of your mom and dad's?" The question had two purposes. One was to distract Becky. If she had something else to think about, she wouldn't have as much time to worry about what Ann might be doing. The other purpose was to find out what Flynn McCallister was doing with a little girl in his apartment. Over the past two years, she'd seen him with a number of women, but none of them looked the type to be mothers.

"I don't have a dad. Me and Mom do just fine without him."

"I'm sure you do. Then Flynn must be a friend of your mom's?" What kind of woman would leave her child in the care of a playboy like McCallister?

"Nope."

Ann's hand stilled a moment. "Well, then, how do you know him?"

"I found him last night."

"You *found* him?"

"Yup."

"How did you find him?" Ann's hand continued to move automatically.

"He sat on me."

"Sat on you?" She was beginning to feel like a parrot, repeating everything Becky said.

"Uh-huh. And then, he said it wasn't fair that he had lots of beds and I didn't have any so I could use one of his beds."

"Wait a minute. He sat on you and then offered you a place to sleep? Where did you meet him?"

"In the alley."

"What alley?" This was starting to sound like a vaudeville routine.

"The one back of this building."

"What were you doing there and what was Flynn doing there?"

"Well, I was sleeping and Mr. Flynn was real drunk. I'm not sure what he was doing there, but after he sat on my foot we came up here. That's when he told me a dragon lived next door, only I don't think you're a dragon. I think you're pretty nice."

"Thank you." Ann applied a small butterfly bandage to the wound, tugging the edges of the cut together. "There. I think you're just about fixed up. We need to wash the blood out of your hair and you'll be just as good as new."

Becky sat up, cautiously fingering the bandage on her head. "It doesn't feel very big." There was an element of disappointment in the words, and Ann hid a grin as she repacked her medical bag. Was there a child anywhere who didn't relish the idea of a big bandage to show off once they were sure the injury itself was taken care of?

"It really wasn't a very big cut, just a nasty one. Don't tug on the bandage and don't get it wet. In a few days we'll take it off and you'll hardly be able to tell that you were ever hurt."

She lifted her head and was surprised to find that Becky was holding out her hand, her small face very solemn. "Thank you, Miss..." Her face scrunched up in thought and then she shook her head. "I can't remember your name."

"Ann. Ann Perry." Since it seemed to be expected of her, Ann took Becky's hand and shook it, biting the inside of her lip to hold back a smile at the quaintly adult gesture. "You're very welcome. I'm glad I was here."

"I've got the water ready. Should I put it in a bowl?"

Flynn stood at the top of the steps, his expression anxious. He looked like a tousled satyr. Three-quarters naked, his hair mussed, his face unshaven. Becky knelt to look over the back of the sofa at him and then she turned to look at Ann, her eyes sparkling with mischief. Ann couldn't help but grin.

"You can put it in the sink."

Flynn frowned. "The sink? That's not very sterile, is it?"

"It doesn't matter."

"Doesn't matter? Shouldn't things that contact an open wound be sterile?"

"It's not going to contact an open wound. We're all done."

"All done? Then what's the boiling water for?"

"You were hovering. I had to give you something to do."

"You mean I boiled that water for nothing?"

"You could make tea."

Becky giggled at Flynn's indignant expression. He glared at Ann a moment longer, well aware that she was enjoying this. Ann gave him her most bland smile, the one she reserved for pushy salesclerks. She was relieved when his eyes shifted to Becky.

"Well, urchin, you certainly look a lot less gruesome than you did a few minutes ago."

"Ann says that in a few days I'll be good as new."

"Why don't we rinse that blood out of your hair and get you a change of clothes and then it will be hard to tell that you've endured a terrible ordeal."

He stepped down into the living room and then grabbed for the towel as it threatened to fall. He flushed, but Ann's face turned scarlet. She was a doctor, she'd seen plenty of naked men, but she had the feeling she wasn't going to be able to put Flynn McCallister in the same category as her patients. She stood up, hoping he wouldn't notice the color in her face.

"Why don't I take care of Becky and you can get some clothes on?"

Flynn hesitated a moment and then looked at Becky. The little girl didn't seem to have any objections to Ann's suggestion. He smiled, and Ann felt her pulse pick up at the sheer beauty of the expression. When he smiled like that, he looked almost angelic. But she doubted that angels had muscles like that.

"Good idea. This towel isn't really the best thing for entertaining. Becky can show you her room. Her clothes are in there and there's a bathroom right next door.''

He disappeared into the hallway. Ann and Becky followed more slowly. The room he'd given Becky was, like the rest of the apartment, beautifully decorated. Everything was of the highest quality. The McCallisters were hardly hurting for money so that wasn't surprising. What was surprising was the empty feel of the room. Not just empty because no one lived there, but empty like something that had once held life and was now drained. Ann felt a shiver run up her spine.

"It's pretty, isn't it?" She looked down at Becky and forced a smile. The word that came to mind was dead, but she could hardly say that to a child.

"Very pretty. Now, where are your clothes? We'll get you cleaned up."

Becky lifted a worn shopping bag onto the bed and carefully took out a stuffed giraffe and set him on the bed. Next came a well-thumbed book and a scuffed jewelry case. The final layer was clothing, folded as neatly as childish hands could manage.

Ann's heart twisted when she realized what she was seeing. This was clearly everything Becky owned in the world. She sat down on the edge of the bed and picked up the giraffe, keeping her head bent over the toy so that Becky wouldn't see the tears in her eyes.

"That's Frankie."

"He's very nice."

"I've had him since I was a baby."

"Did your mother give him to you?"

Becky hesitated a minute and then shook her head. "I think Daddy gave him to me."

Ann fingered the distinctive button in the toy's ear and filed away that bit of information.

"Daddy gave me this book, too."

Ann set the stuffed toy down and picked up the book. It was *A Child's Garden of Verses*, a beautiful leather-bound edition, old and much worn, showing the love of more than one generation.

"Was this your daddy's when he was a little boy?"

"I don't know. Mama doesn't much like to talk about him." She took the book from Ann and set it next to the giraffe, clearly saying that the subject was closed. Ann accepted her lead, knowing that you didn't win a child's confidence by pushing.

"Is this all your clothes?"

"Most of 'em. When Mama comes home we're going to go shopping. She says I'm growing like a weed."

Ann nodded and picked up a pair of jeans and a long-sleeved blue shirt. There wasn't a whole lot of choice. Other than the garments in her hand, there was one other pair of jeans with the knees worn out and a short-sleeved pullover that looked too small.

"Well, let's get you changed and your hair washed."

Becky chattered confidently while Ann rinsed her hair, careful to keep the wound dry. There was a hair dryer in the bathroom cabinet, and it took only a few minutes to dry the little girl's hair. Ann borrowed a bobby pin from her own hair and pinned Becky's fine bangs back away from her face.

Looking in the bathroom mirror, she was aware that her neat chignon was beginning to look more than a little scruffy. She pushed at a few straggling strands, but there wasn't really much she could do. Not that it mattered what she looked like. Becky didn't care and Flynn McCallister's opinion was less than important.

Ann and Becky were in the living room, standing by the balcony doors when Flynn entered from the hall. He'd taken time to finish his interrupted shower, but he hadn't bothered to shave. Wearing a pair of jeans that were just snug enough to be interesting and a blue chambray shirt that he was still buttoning, he looked distressingly attractive.

It was pure dislike that made her feel slightly breathless. It had nothing to do with an urge to lay her palm against his chest and see if the hair felt as crisp as it looked. It had nothing to do with the way his shirt clung to his damp skin, outlining every muscle. It was nothing but dislike.

"Becky, why don't you go out and take a look at the plants on the balcony. I want to talk to Flynn."

Flynn stopped a few feet away and looked at her, one dark brow arching in question. Becky looked from one to the other and her pale brows puckered.

"Are you going to fight?"

"No."

"Maybe."

Ann flashed Flynn a quelling look that didn't appear to faze him in the least. "We're not going to fight, Becky. We're just going to talk."

Becky looked at Flynn, clearly more willing to trust his judgment than Ann's. "Go on out, urchin. There's some hand tools in the box next to the door. Why don't you dig in one of the empty planters. I promise we're not going to come to blows."

The late summer sun was low in the sky, but it would be another hour or more before the light was gone. The upper floor of the building was smaller than the floors below, allowing for a large roof garden for each apartment. Ann hired professional gardeners to care for her garden. It was lovely, not a leaf out of place, and she seldom paid any attention to it. Flynn's garden was considerably less neat. Plants sprawled wherever their fancy took them. Some of the planters were empty, while others held such a wealth of vegetation, it was hard to distinguish one plant from another. It was the perfect place for a child to play. She watched Becky disappear into the jungle of growth, trowel in hand.

The smile that softened her mouth disappeared when she turned to look at Flynn. "I think we need to have a talk, Mr. McCallister."

That irritating brow arched. "Call me Flynn. It's much easier to get out when you're yelling at someone."

"I have no intention—"

"Sure you do. I recognize the look. My mother tried calling me Mr. McCallister when she was angry. She thought it might have more impact but then my father would think she was yelling at him and he'd get mad at her and...well, you can see how much simpler it is if you just call me Flynn. Would you like some coffee? Don't tell Becky, but her coffee is a potential weapon."

He moved toward the kitchen, leaving Ann no choice but to follow. She wasn't quite sure he'd done it, but somehow he'd managed to take control of the situation from her.

In the kitchen, he began making coffee and Ann made an effort to bring the conversation back to where it belonged.

"I don't want any coffee, thank you. I want to talk about Becky."

"It's your loss. I make an excellent cup of coffee."

"I don't care about coffee. I want to talk about that little girl." When he glanced at her this time, his mouth had quirked to match the eyebrow, making Ann aware that her voice had risen. She wasn't shouting but she was perilously close. She took a deep breath, drawing on her considerable self-control and forced her voice to a calm level.

"I think there are some questions that need to be answered."

"Ask away." Since the invitation was punctuated by his turning on the coffee grinder, Ann had doubts about his sincerity. She waited until the machine had stopped running and then continued as if the interruption hadn't occurred.

"I'd like to know just what Becky is doing here."

He poured the coffee into the filter and turned to look at her as if he questioned her sanity. "She's playing on the balcony."

Ann ground her teeth together. The man was being deliberately obtuse and infuriating. She knew he was doing it deliberately, but it didn't seem to curb the rapid climb of her blood pressure.

"Mr. McCallister, I'm willing to stand here all night and play word games with you but it's not going to do either of us any good. I'm concerned about that child and I am going to get the answers I want."

Flynn poured water into the coffee maker and then leaned one leg against the counter and studied her. Ann felt a flush come up in her cheeks. She didn't have to look at herself to know what he was seeing. Her hair was coming down around her ears, her suit jacket was gone, her blouse was undone at the throat, her skirt was probably wrinkled and, to top it off, she wasn't wearing shoes. She made a less than imposing figure and she knew it.

Whether it was the determined set of her chin or something else that only he saw, Flynn seemed to make up his mind to cooperate, at least up to a point.

"I haven't said thank-you for what you did for Becky. I'm not sure who was more frightened, her or me. I really appreciate the way you came over here and patched her up."

"You're welcome. It is my job."

"Not when you're off duty. I'm truly grateful."

"It really wasn't that big a deal." *Damn the man!* Just when she thought she had control of the situation, he did something to throw her off balance again. Did he have to sound so sincere?

"It was a big deal to Becky and me." The coffee maker pinged, and he turned and got two cups down out of the cupboard. He filled them with coffee and handed one to Ann. "If you don't want it, I'll drink it. Let's go into the living room and get comfortable. We can keep an eye on the balcony from there."

Once again, she found herself trailing after him, not quite sure how he'd managed to turn the situation around. Somehow, the edge of her anger had been blunted. She settled onto an off-white overstuffed chair and then realized it was a tactical error. The chair didn't just invite you to sit back and relax, it insisted that you do so. The huge puffy cushions practically swallowed her. There was no way she could use any effective body language in this chair. On the other hand, she couldn't change seats without looking like an idiot. She shot Flynn an annoyed look, wondering if he'd done this deliberately, but he'd settled into an identical chair and managed to look completely in command of himself, the furniture and the situation. Ann felt like a little girl sitting in her father's chair. She could barely move to set her coffee cup down on an end table—the coffee she hadn't wanted, she remembered irritably.

"What did you want to talk about?"

"Becky."

"What about her?" His eyes were cool and watchful.

"I want to know what she's doing here. And don't tell me that she's playing on the balcony. She said that you found her in the alley last night and offered her a bed. Is that true?"

"Pretty much."

"How could you!"

"You think it would have been better to leave her in the alley?"

"That's not what I mean!"

"Then what did you mean?"

"Mr. McCallister—"

"Flynn. It's much easier to spit out."

Ann ground her teeth together. "Flynn. Didn't it occur to you that her mother would be worried about her? You should have contacted her immediately. I've always known that you were irresponsible but I wouldn't have believed that even you would do something like this. That poor woman must be out of her mind with worry."

"You've always known that I was irresponsible? You must have amazing powers of observation, Ms. Perry. Considering that your only contact with me over the past two years has been a few barbs exchanged in the hallway. On what do you base this sweeping judgment?"

Ann opened her mouth but he cut her off with a sharp gesture. "I don't really want to hear it. Your opinion of me is neither here nor there. Becky's mother disappeared two weeks ago. The landlady was about to turn Becky over to Social Services. Becky is terrified of them so she ran away. She's been living on the streets for the past few days. No matter how irresponsible I am, I think I'm a better bet than the streets."

"That's not the issue."

"Just what is the issue, Ms. Perry? Do you think I'm going to corrupt her?"

He was backing her into a corner and she didn't like the feeling. Somehow, he'd managed to put her in the wrong. She felt trapped—physically and verbally.

"She says you were intoxicated last night."

"Smashed to the gills."

"You can't possibly think that's a good influence for a child."

"I don't think it's going to put a permanent warp on her psyche to see a man drunk."

"The fact that you drink to excess doesn't make you a particularly good guardian for a child, even temporarily."

"I do not drink to excess on a regular basis."

Ann flushed angrily at the prissy tone he used to repeat her words. "I suppose last night was a special occasion."

"In a manner of speaking. It was my brother's birthday."

"And that's supposed to make it all right? The two of you go out and—"

"Not the two of us. I was alone. Mark died three years ago."

Ann wondered if it were possible to coax the huge chair into swallowing her completely. "I'm sorry."

There was a moment of silence and then Flynn ran his fingers through his hair. The crooked smile he gave her was half apology and wholly charming.

"I'm the one who should be sorry. I know you're concerned about Becky and I shouldn't be giving you such a hard time."

"She can't just continue to stay here. You've got to let someone know where she is. Maybe the Social Services people *should* be called." The suggestion was made without force.

"No. Becky's terrified of them. Probably with good reason. There are some pretty flaky sounding circumstances surrounding her mother. They just might take Becky away from her."

"Then, what are you going to do?"

He rubbed his forehead and Ann noticed his pallor for the first time.

"Either I'm getting too old to drink like that or hangovers are getting worse. I'm not sure what I'm going to do about Becky. I thought I'd take her out to my parents' home tomorrow. They may have some ideas. You're welcome to come along just to make sure that I don't sell her to the white slavers." He grinned to show her that there was no rancor behind the words.

Of course she wasn't going to get involved any further. It was none of her business what happened to either of them. She'd done all that could be expected of her. Naturally, she would turn down his invitation. She was going to get out of her chair and say a polite good-night—she'd even wish him luck—and then she was going to go back to her own apartment and her simple, uncomplicated life. The only male she wanted to deal with right now was Oscar, who didn't have any of the dangerous seductive qualities of Flynn McCallister.

"If you wouldn't mind, I'd feel better seeing this a little farther. I don't know why. I hardly know Becky."

"There's something about her that sort of gets under your skin."

Ann nodded, suppressing the thought that Becky might not be the only one.

Chapter Four

"Are you sure you don't want another piece of pizza, Mr. Flynn?"

Flynn stared at the slice of pizza Becky was holding out and swallowed hard. Red with tomato sauce and dripping with cheese, it couldn't have looked more deadly to him if it had been laced with cyanide.

"No thanks. You two go ahead and split it." One thing he'd forgotten about hangovers was that, no matter how bad you felt when you woke up, you could count on it being the best you'd feel all day.

He pushed his chair back from the table, as much to get away from the food as to get more comfortable, and studied his companions. Twenty-four hours ago, he'd never have believed that he'd be sitting across the table from one small refugee and one hostile neighbor. To tell the truth, the refugee was easier to imagine than Ann. Who would have believed that the dragon across the hall would have such a pretty smile?

He looked at Becky, his face softening. She'd lost the wary look she'd had just a few short hours ago. She seemed completely at home. Tomorrow he'd have to figure out what to do with her, but for tonight, he just wanted her to be a child. He had the feeling that she'd spent too little time doing that.

"Parcheesi." Ann and Becky looked at him. Becky looked intrigued; Ann looked suspicious. He grinned at them both. "What we need is a nice game of Parcheesi before bed."

"I don't think—"

"I love Parcheesi."

Ann swallowed the rest of her protest and managed to look enthused. Board games were right below jogging on her list of fun things to do. She'd never understood why people thought it was fun to move little pieces of plastic around a sheet of cardboard. In her experience, it led to arguments and irritation and hurt feelings. But then she'd never played with Flynn McCallister.

Over the next two hours, she learned that not everyone was like her father, who went about playing a game the way he went about life—you were there to win and nothing else mattered. Flynn didn't seem to think that winning was all that important. His only goal was to have fun, and he took just as much pleasure in losing as he did in winning. He coached Becky, he coached Ann, and he didn't seem to care that they trounced him every time.

It was a novel experience and one that wasn't entirely welcome. She didn't want to like Flynn. Not only had she grown accustomed to their antagonistic relationship over the past two years—she felt safe with it. Something told her that Flynn McCallister might be dangerous if he got any closer than arm's length. She wasn't quite sure just how he'd be dangerous, but she didn't doubt that the danger was real.

After four games of Parcheesi, both adults called a halt to any further games. Becky looked as if she'd like to protest, but didn't feel confident enough of her position to argue. Flynn ruffled her hair as he put the lid on the game box.

"We'll play again, urchin. And next time, I won't go so easy on the two of you."

"Does that mean you're not going to lose every game, Mr. Flynn?"

Ann couldn't help but grin at the way the little girl got straight to the point. Flynn gave her a stern look but she could see the laughter in his eyes. She couldn't remember ever knowing someone who could laugh at themselves so readily. Was there anything that he took seriously?

"That means I'm not going to lose every game." He slid the game onto the top shelf of a cupboard and Ann tried not to notice the way his jeans molded to his thighs. The man was just too attractive to be safe.

"Time for a bath, I think." He rubbed his forehead as he spoke and, for the first time in hours, Ann remembered that he'd spent the better part of the previous night drinking.

Against her will, she felt sorry for him. She'd never had a hangover herself but it couldn't be pleasant. No matter how much she disapproved of his drinking, she couldn't help but take pity on him. If his head was hurting as much as she suspected, he could use a short break from his role as host and baby-sitter.

"Why don't I help you with your bath, Becky? I want to be sure you keep that bandage dry."

Ann ignored the grateful glance Flynn threw her. She didn't want him to get the idea that she was doing this for him. When she and Becky returned to the living room, Flynn was looking a little less pale, but Ann told herself that she only noticed because her medical training made it impossible to ignore.

He smiled at Becky, but his eyes skimmed over her and Ann knew he'd seen the threadbare condition of her pajamas. He didn't say anything that might hurt Becky's pride.

"Ready for bed?"

"I'm not tired." A yawn punctuated the end of the sentence and Ann saw Flynn bite his lip against a smile.

"Well, Ann and I are very tired so why don't you humor us and hop into bed. You can sleep in the room you had last night."

"Okay." She turned away and then looked over her shoulder at him. "Are you going to tuck me in?" The question was hesitant, as if she were afraid he'd refuse.

"I wouldn't miss it for the world. We'll both tuck you in."

Lying in the huge bed, the covers tucked under her chin, Becky's youth and fragility were more apparent than ever. She was such a plucky little thing that it was easy to forget just how young she was.

Flynn sat on the edge of the bed and brushed the hair back from her forehead. "Tomorrow, we're going to go visit my parents and we'll decide what to do about you."

"You won't give me to the welfare, will you?" Her thin fingers came up to clutch his hand.

"I won't give you to the welfare people. I promise. But we've got to decide how to go about finding your mom. She's going to be worried about you when she gets home and you're not there."

Ann moved to sit on the other side of the bed. "I'm going to go with you to visit Flynn's parents."

"We'll have a great time." Flynn brushed the hair back from Becky's face and smiled at her. Ann was stunned to feel a twinge of envy. She wanted that smile turned her way. The realization was so surprising that she almost got up and ran out of the apartment, as if getting away from him was the only way to protect herself. But protect herself from what?

"Could you tell me a story, Mr. Flynn? Mama always tells me a story 'fore bedtime."

Ann barely listened as he began to spin a story full of the requisite number of dragons and princesses and handsome princes. She didn't want to hear the soft rise and fall of his voice. She didn't want to see the way his eyes softened when he looked at Becky. She didn't want to like him. It wasn't safe.

She was so absorbed in her thoughts that she jumped when he touched her arm. Her eyes focused on his face and then quickly shifted away, afraid that he might be able to see her confused thoughts. Becky was fast asleep, her lashes lying in soft crescents against her cheeks. She didn't stir as the two adults eased themselves off the bed and tiptoed out of the room.

Flynn stopped in the middle of the living room and turned to look at her. He ran his fingers through his hair, ruffling it into thick black waves.

"You can stay the night if it would make you feel better. There's plenty of room."

"No." The word came out too stark, too revealing. She cleared her throat and tried again. "I don't think there's any need for that. I'll just come over in the morning." She edged toward the door. "What time are you thinking of leaving?"

"Sometime after I get up and I have a feeling that, with Becky around, that's not going to be terribly late." He smiled crookedly. "I suspect she's an early riser."

"Probably. Most children seem to be." She edged a little closer to the door. "Well, I guess I'll go home now."

Flynn followed her to the door and Ann was vividly aware of him every step of the way. He reached around her to flip the lock, and it took all her control to keep from shying away from him. If he noticed her tension, he was polite enough not to mention it.

Ann stepped into the hall, feeling as if she were escaping some fatal temptation. "I'll see you tomorrow, then." Reluctantly, she turned to look at him, resisting the urge to run for the haven of her own apartment.

He nodded, stifling a yawn. "Sorry. I guess I'm getting too old for all-night binges. I'll come knock on your door around ten. That should give us plenty of time to get out to my parents' house by lunchtime. My mother puts on a great spread."

"That sounds fine." Ann was aware of him watching her until she opened her own door. She turned, lifting her hand in what she hoped was a casual gesture. "Good night."

"Good night."

She shut the door as quickly as seemed polite, slumping back against the sturdy wood. Oscar looked up from his favorite spot on the hall table, his yellow eyes full of polite inquiry.

"Oh, Oscar. What have I gotten myself into?"

BY THE TIME FLYNN'S CAR pulled into the long driveway of his parents' estate outside Santa Barbara, Ann had convinced herself that her nervousness of the night before was a product of an overtired mind and an overactive imagination. Flynn McCallister was attractive, there was no denying that, but he was also a playboy who seemed to be content to drift through life. She could never be seriously drawn to a man like that.

And, if her heartbeat showed a tendency to accelerate when he was near, that was just hormones. Easily understood and easily controlled.

"Is that where your mom and dad live?" Becky's awed question broke the silence in the Ferrari.

Flynn nodded as he pulled the sleek car to a halt in front of the door. "This is where I grew up."

"It's beautiful."

Flynn studied the building, trying to see it through Becky's eyes. The house was built along the lines of an antebellum mansion, complete with a wide veranda and sturdy pillars across the front. When he was growing up there, it had just been home.

"I suppose it is."

The door to the house opened as Ann got out of the car and lifted Becky off her lap and onto the gravel drive. The woman who came down the steps was short and elegantly slim. Her dark hair was going gray without any pretensions, and her blue eyes were a much paler reflection of her son's.

Flynn came around the front of the car, his long strides covering the distance between them, catching his mother around the waist and lifting her off the bottom step. She laughed, a girlish sound that made Ann smile. "Put me down, hooligan." He obeyed, his wide smile matching hers. She examined her son with maternal eyes, finally reaching up to pat his cheek.

"We don't see you often enough, Flynn. Your father thought you might call this week."

"Because of Mark's birthday?" His smile twisted. "I celebrated in my own way."

"I know but your father was a bit upset."

"So what else is new? Mom, I want you to meet Ann Perry, my neighbor, and this is Becky Sinclair. I told you about her on the phone. Ann, Becky, this is Louise McCallister, my mother."

The smile Louise turned on Ann and Becky was warm and full of welcome. "I'm so pleased to meet both of you. We're having a late lunch today so you'll have time to rest a bit after the drive from L.A. You must have been crowded in that little sports car. Why didn't you drive the Mercedes, Flynn?"

"Becky preferred the Ferrari, Mom."

"Actually, it wasn't very crowded at all, Mrs. McCallister. Becky doesn't take up much room."

"Call me Louise. Come in and meet my husband."

Ann followed her hostess up the steps, aware of Flynn following behind with Becky. Becky seemed a bit awestruck by the elegant house, and her hand clung to Flynn's. The interior of the house was as polished as the exterior. Dark mahogany floors and creamy wallpaper created a rich background for the beautiful antiques that filled the hallway.

Ann's father was a wealthy man and she'd grown up around money. But there was something different here, some indefinable essence. The McCallister home smelled of old money—lots of it. The walls seemed permeated with quiet elegance. Some of the antiques were one of a kind pieces—all of them were exquisite.

Despite the decor, it wasn't difficult to imagine Flynn and his brother growing up here. Beneath the rich beauty, the big house felt like a home. A place where two growing boys could have laughed and played without restrictions.

Louise led the way across the hall and into the study where her husband awaited them. The man who stood to greet them was not at all what Ann had expected. She hadn't given much conscious thought to what Flynn's father would be like, but she'd had a vague image of an older version of Flynn—tall, lean, with elegantly masculine grace.

She hadn't expected a stocky man a few inches short of six feet. His features were blunt, his eyes a clear, sharp gray rather than electric blue. The only resemblance she could see was the thick black hair, now heavily streaked with gray.

His handshake was firm, his look direct, lacking the lazy charm that made his son so fascinating and so exasperating.

"Thank you for allowing me to come, Mr. Mc-Callister."

"I don't blame you for not trusting Flynn with the child. My son isn't known for his sense of responsibility." Ann blinked, wondering if she'd misunderstood him, wondering what she was supposed to say in reply if she hadn't.

"Hello, Dad. Nice to know that some things never change. It's great to see you again, too." There was an edge to Flynn's voice. "Ann, this is my father."

David McCallister nodded to his son, his eyes cool. "Flynn. I thought you might call this week."

"So Mom told me. You know how I always hate to do the expected. Besides, we would have quarreled and that seems like a hell of a way to honor Mark's birth-day." His tone closed the subject and there was an uncomfortable silence in the room.

It was Louise who broke it, her expression deter-minedly cheerful. "Becky, I think the cook was mak-ing some cookies this morning. Why don't I take you to the kitchen. I don't think one or two cookies is likely to spoil your lunch."

Becky pressed tighter to Flynn's leg, her eyes wide and uncertain. "I'd like to stay with Mr. Flynn, please."

Flynn sank down to her level, meeting her eyes. "It's okay, honey. Go ahead and go with my mom. I promise I won't disappear without you. We have some things we need to talk about. Grown-up things."

"Are you going to talk about me?"

"Yes. But that's nothing to worry about. We're just going to decide what to do about finding your mother."

"You won't call the welfare, will you?"

"I already told you I would't do that, didn't I? Now, go have some cookies but make sure you save some for me."

He stood up, ruffling her hair. Becky hesitated a moment longer, looking from Flynn to his mother's outstretched hand, and then she moved forward and tentatively placed her small fingers in Louise's palm.

"Are they chocolate chip cookies?"

"I don't know. Why don't we go see?" Ann watched Louise lead the little girl from the room and swallowed an unexpected lump in her throat. No matter what else he was, there was no denying that Flynn was very good with Becky. He showed an understanding of her fears and uncertainties Ann had to admit she couldn't have matched herself.

The door shut behind Louise and Becky and silence descended. At first it wasn't uncomfortable. Ann had never felt that every second had to be filled with talk. She looked around the room, admiring the walls of books, most of them leather bound. One shelf held trophies, another—family photographs. It was a warm room, full of leather and wood. There was a huge bowl of flowers on a table near the door, and the brilliant colors were a perfect accent to the muted tones of the room.

Having looked at the room, she began to notice how the silence had lengthened. She looked at Flynn, who sat in a chair, his long legs stretched out in front of him. His expression was brooding, his attention all for the toes of his sneakers.

His father sat in a chair not far away, but Flynn might not have been there for all the attention the man paid him. He was staring out the window, his face set in bitter lines, his stocky body held rigidly upright against the soft leather of the chair.

Since no one seemed interested in speaking, she moved over to the photos, studying them with an interest that surprised her. It wasn't hard to identify the family members. A younger Louise, her expression as warm as it was now. Her husband, his face a little less stern, his eyes softer. There was a stocky young man who showed up in most of the photos, which must've been Mark. She examined his face, liking the warmth and humor that lit his eyes. There seemed to be a vague melancholy in his eyes, but that could have been her imagination.

And there was Flynn. His lean body lanky with youth and then gradually filling out but retaining that graceful look that was so much a part of his attraction today.

She looked at the photos again, a little uneasy with what she was seeing. There were numerous photos of Mark as football captain in his uniform, at the beach and in almost every other setting. Flynn was in some of the pictures, sometimes in the background, sometimes with his arm over his older brother's shoulder. But there were no photos of Flynn alone. The realization sank in gradually and Ann turned away from the pictures, not wanting to think about the implications of what she was seeing. She didn't want to feel sympathy for Flynn McCallister. He was dangerous enough without adding that emotional complication.

The silence had stretched out behind her, making an almost visible presence in the big room. She cleared her throat.

"You have a lovely home, Mr. McCallister. Flynn tells me he grew up here."

His eyes snapped to her, dark and fierce. "He and his brother Mark both grew up here. Did he mention his brother?"

Ann glanced at Flynn, but he didn't shift his eyes from his shoes. She was on her own. "Flynn told me that his brother died three years ago. That must have been a terrible time for all of you."

"My son Mark was a wonderful boy. He was a police officer. Did Flynn tell you that? Died in the line of duty."

"I didn't know that. You must have been very proud of him."

"I was." He glanced at Flynn without speaking, and his son's eyes came up to meet his. From where Ann sat, there was absolutely no readable expression in his face. Father and son stared at each other across an abyss that had obviously been there for a very long time. Flynn smiled, the insolent smile that Ann had seen so often the past two years, the smile that said he didn't give a damn about the rest of the world.

"Hey, Dad, don't feel too bad. One out of two ain't bad."

The older man's face darkened, and Ann braced herself for the explosion that was sure to follow. She'd seen that look in her own father's eyes too often to mistake it. Why had Flynn provoked him?

The explosion didn't come. She didn't even know if it would have come, because the door opened and Louise stepped into the room. Ann felt as if she'd been thrown a life jacket in the midst of a stormy sea. The older woman's eyes took in the situation immediately, and Ann caught a glimpse of her distress before she set about pouring oil on the waters.

"Are you two at it again? Can't you see you're embarrassing Ann? She's going to think you're a pair of ill-mannered fools. Would you like some lemonade, my dear? Becky is settled in the kitchen and Maggie is teaching her how to bake cookies. I think lunch may be a little late.

"What a charming child. I'm so glad you brought her to see us, Flynn. Exactly what would you like us to do for her?"

The next few hours passed on a more calm note, though Ann had the feeling that the hostilities lay just beneath the surface, ready to break out again. Even when the McCallister men agreed on something, it was grudgingly, as if each were reluctant to admit that the other might have had a good idea. By the time Becky's immediate future was hammered out, Ann felt as if she'd witnessed a battle between the superpowers.

It was agreed that Becky's terror of the welfare department eliminated the possibility of calling the authorities. On the other hand, something had to be done about finding her mother. It was Flynn's suggestion that they call a private detective and, very reluctantly, his father agreed that it seemed like a reasonable alternative. The major disagreement came when the discussion turned to what to do with Becky while the detective searched for her mother.

"Obviously, the child will stay with your mother and I." David McCallister's bluff voice said there would be no argument. Ann felt herself quail at the tone. It was so familiar. Just the way her father always sounded when he was laying down the law.

Flynn did not seem impressed.

"I don't think so. Becky is doing just fine at my place. I don't see any reason why she shouldn't just continue to stay with me until her mother is found."

"Don't be ridiculous. You've got no business being in charge of a little girl. What do you know about children?"

Flynn eyes were sapphire blue and just as hard. "I know that you have to give them room to grow and you have to love them for what they are, not for what you want them to be."

"That's enough, Flynn." Louise's quiet voice discharged the explosion that was building. Flynn pulled his gaze from his father's angry face and glanced at his mother before looking at Ann. He lifted his shoulders in an apologetic shrug, his mouth a cynical line.

"Sorry. We shouldn't drag you into old family quarrels."

"That's okay." But it wasn't okay. She could see the pain in his eyes and she was surprised to find that she ached in sympathy. She had the strangest urge to stroke the tousled hair back off his forehead and hold him close until the pain left his eyes. She dragged her gaze away from him, frightened by the strength of the urge.

The thought slipped into her mind that it was safer to be hostile to Flynn McCallister. He was a dangerous man to care about.

Once again, it was Louise who brought the conversation back to a more comfortable level.

"We're discussing Becky's welfare here and I think the least we can do is keep that in mind." Her stern gaze took in both her husband and her son. Her husband grunted and looked away. Flynn gave her an unabashed grin.

"You're quite right, Mom. *We* do need to keep that in mind. So what do you suggest?"

"Why don't we ask Becky?" Ann made the suggestion hesitantly, wondering if perhaps she was sticking her nose in where it didn't belong. But she was supposed to be here to help decide Becky's future.

The three McCallisters looked at her with varying degrees of surprise. Louise spoke first.

"What a wonderful idea. I don't know why we didn't think of that right away. Thank you, Ann."

"I love a woman who can think in the midst of battle. Remind me to kiss you first chance I get." Ann flushed, uncomfortably aware that the idea of him kissing her was not as unpleasant as it should be. In fact, it wasn't unpleasant at all.

"You can't expect a child to make a decision like that." David McCallister was the only dissenting voice.

"Why not?" Flynn's question held insolent challenge, all the laughing approval he'd shown Ann gone as if it had never been. His mother rushed into speech, intent on averting a scene.

"Becky seems like a very levelheaded little girl. I think she has a right to have some say in her future. I'll go get her now." She got up and left the room with quick steps, cutting off the possibility of further argument.

The three left behind sat in silence for the short time she was gone. Flynn's father stared into space. Flynn looked at Ann and Ann looked at the toes of her shoes, unwilling to meet those bright blue eyes, uneasy with the way her pulse seemed to respond to the warmth of his gaze. It seemed as if hours had gone by, but it was no more than a minute or two before Louise returned with Becky.

The two of them had barely entered the room before Becky tugged her hand loose from the older woman's and ran to Flynn's side. Flynn slid his arm around her waist as she leaned against his knee. Looking at the two of them, Ann already knew Becky's answer.

"How were the cookies, urchin?"

"They were great and Maggie let me help her take them off the pan. Could we make cookies when we get home, Mr. Flynn?"

"Sure. But first, we've got a question to ask you." She caught the serious tone of his voice and stared at him, gray eyes wide with uncertainty.

"We're going to hire someone to look for your mom but, until they find her, you need a place to stay."

"Can't I stay with you?" Her voice quivered slightly and Flynn hugged her reassuringly.

"Sure you can, honey. But my parents have said that you can stay here if you want. There's lots of room to play here and I could come out and visit you." He was scrupulously honest in his presentation of the choice but it was clear that, as far as Becky was concerned, there was no choice to be made.

"Do you want me to stay here, Mr. Flynn? Am I too much trouble for you?"

"Of course not, Becky. I'd love to have you with me. But my parents would love to have you here, too. The choice is up to you."

"I want to stay with you, please."

To his credit, Flynn did not give his father a triumphant look. "I'd like that, too."

"MARK AND I USED TO PLAY on those swings. I bet they haven't been used since we were kids." Flynn waved at Becky who was happily absorbed in pumping herself as high as possible.

Lunch had passed without incident and they had been invited to stay to dinner. It was clear that Flynn hadn't wanted to stay but had agreed for his mother's sake and he'd escaped outside as soon as possible, taking Ann and Becky with him. Ann wasn't sorry to get away from the tension that stretched between the men in the family.

It was a beautiful day and the grounds that surrounded the house invited casual strolling. Flynn bent and picked up a stick, tossing it to the elderly retriever who'd followed them from the house. She sniffed at the stick and then looked at Flynn as if to say that he was very foolish if he didn't realize that she was long past the age to chase sticks. "Sorry, Bessy. I forgot."

She yawned once and then turned to make her way toward the house, her steps slightly stiff with age but her dignity unruffled. Flynn watched her cross the wide expanse of lawn that lay between them and the house and then turned back to Ann.

"I can remember when Bessy would beg me to throw sticks for her. I guess I haven't gotten home much these last few years. I tend to forget how old she's getting."

"You and your father don't get along very well, do you?" Ann hadn't planned on asking the question. It was none of her business, and she didn't want to become any more involved with Flynn and his family than she already was. Nevertheless, there the question was and, once asked, she wanted to hear his answer.

"A masterpiece of understatement if I've ever heard one." Flynn's voice was heavy with sarcasm. "My father thinks I'm a playboy and a wastrel. I haven't done any of the things a McCallister is supposed to do. As far as he's concerned, I haven't done anything right since I was born."

Ann stared at Becky without seeing her. Flynn's words brought back her own childhood too vividly for comfort. "It must have been hard to please him."

Flynn shrugged. "I never tried. At least I quit trying so long ago that I can't remember it ever being different."

"How can you not try to please your father?" The concept was so foreign to her that it was as if he were speaking another language.

"I suppose I might have been more inclined to try if it hadn't been for my older brother. You see, Mark was perfect. My father didn't just *think* he was perfect, he really was." His smile twisted with memories. "He was captain of his football team, captain of the debating team. I swear, in kindergarten, he started out as captain of the clean-up squad. He got straight A's right from the start. He was intelligent, polite, handsome and had a great sense of humor."

He reached out and tugged on a pendulous eucalyptus branch, methodically stripping it of every leaf.

"The awful thing about Mark was that it was all absolutely sincere. He was truly the greatest older brother any kid could want."

"But you couldn't compete." Ann's voice was soft. She knew just how he felt, though her competition had been the ideal of a son who'd never existed outside her father's dreams.

"I couldn't compete." He finished with the branch and reached for another one. "I gave up trying even before I got into school. I don't know, I sometimes think I became a rebel just to give myself an identity. At least Dad noticed me as something other than Mark's shadow. But maybe that's making myself a little too sympathetic. I can't say I don't enjoy doing exactly what I'm doing. The fact that it irritates Dad is just a side effect."

"Just what do you do?" He slanted her an amused look and Ann flushed, realizing how critical the question sounded. "I mean, you don't seem to go to work or anything...." She trailed off, aware that she hadn't done a very good job of explaining what she meant. Maybe it was because she wasn't entirely sure herself.

"That's okay. Not many people recognize my profession."

He released the branch, letting it snap back into place. The smile he turned on her was brilliant. Ann blinked, not wanting to notice how her heartbeat accelerated under that look.

"Your profession?" She was barely aware of speaking. Was it possible to get lost in a man's eyes?

"I'm a professional playboy. There aren't many of us left in the world. Our numbers have been decimated by increasing social pressures to be useful and develop careers. I'm one of the last of a dying breed. The truly useless man about town." He bowed low before her, and Ann had to bite her lip to hold back a giggle.

"I think you're too hard on yourself. Nobody is completely useless."

"I am. And proud of it."

"Don't you get bored?"

"No. There's so much to see in the world. I travel quite a bit. There's never a chance to get bored."

She shook her head, unable to imagine a life without the limits of work or school to frame the days. "I can't imagine not having a job."

"That's the trouble with the world today. Nobody can imagine life without jobs."

Silence fell between them, not uncomfortable but full of an awareness Ann didn't want to acknowledge. There was something about him that disturbed

her in ways she didn't understand. He was so...
different. She'd never known anyone like him.

"Hold still." His voice was hushed and Ann froze
as he reached toward her. She felt his hand in her hair
and when he pulled away, there was a ladybug resting
on the tip of his finger. "She was tangled in your
hair."

He held his hand up and blew gently. The tiny in-
sect hesitated a moment and then flew away. The
shadow of the big eucalyptus wrapped around them.
The late summer air was still warm. The scent of the
rose garden drifted on the air, a faint hint of perfume.

"You know, for a dragon, you're pretty nice."
Flynn's hand came up to tug at a lock of hair that had
escaped from her braid, but he lingered, his finger
twisted the fiery strand as if tangled in the warmth of
its color. "I've always wondered what your hair would
look like down." The tone was causal, but there was
nothing casual about the way he was looking at her.

"It just looks like hair." Ann told herself she was
imagining the breathlessness in her voice.

"I bet it's beautiful."

His head was lowering toward hers, that brilliant
blue gaze on her mouth. Her lips were suddenly dry
and her tongue came out to wet them, a nervous flicker
of movement. She saw his eyes darken and then his
hand was slipping around the back of her neck, holding her still. But Ann couldn't have moved if her life
depended on it.

His mouth touched hers and her eyelids fell shut as
if attached to weights. She stood as if turned to stone,

her hands clenched into fists at her sides, her head tilted to accept his kiss.

His mouth was warm and dry. She could smell the faint tang of after-shave. Her lips softened under his coaxing and his hand tightened on the back of her neck, tilting her head farther up. Ann's breath caught as his teeth sank gently into her lower lip. Her mouth opened the smallest amount and the kiss deepened. Their breath mingled until it was impossible to tell where one began and the other ended.

Flynn's free hand settled on her lower back as he stepped closer, and Ann's fingers unclenched, her hands creeping up to rest on his shoulders, her movements tentative.

There was a warmth in the pit of her belly. A warmth that had nothing to do with the weather. Her toes curled inside her shoes as his tongue brushed ever so lightly against her lower lip. She could feel something waiting just out of reach. Something exciting and dangerous and full of promise. Something she wasn't sure she was ready to reach for.

"Mr. Flynn."

The voice seemed to come from a long way away. At first Ann couldn't even make sense of what it was saying.

"Mr. Flyyynnn."

Her eyes opened slowly as Flynn's mouth left hers. In his eyes she could see some of the same surprise she was feeling. Her hands dropped away from his shoulders but he was slower to release her. They stared at each other for a few seconds, neither of them quite sure what to say.

"Mr. Flyyynnn." Becky's high-pitched call wafted toward them and Flynn's hands dropped away from Ann. She took a step back, dragging her eyes away from his face. Whatever had just happened, she wasn't ready to examine it.

"Becky wants you. I . . . ah . . . I think I'll go see if I can do something to help your mother with dinner. Set the table or something."

She walked away before he could say anything, but she was aware of his eyes following her until she turned a corner and was shielded by the bulk of the house.

Louise McCallister looked up as Ann all but scuttled into the room. Her face was flushed and there was a distracted expression in her eyes as if she weren't quite sure where she was or how she came to be there.

"Flynn is with Becky. I thought I might be able to help you with dinner."

Louise bit her lip to conceal a smile and bent her head over her needlepoint. "That's very sweet of you, my dear, but I think Maggie has everything well in hand."

"Of course. How foolish of me."

"Not at all. Why don't you join me in a cup of tea?" She poured the fragrant liquid into a Limoges cup, setting it on the edge of the tea table as Ann sat in the chair across from her.

"Did you enjoy your walk?"

"Yes, the grounds are lovely." Ann picked up her tea cup, and Louise politely pretended not to notice the faint tremor that made the delicate cup rattle in its saucer.

"My husband's mother started the landscaping but I've added to it over the years. It's an ongoing job, of course, but I enjoy it. Have you known Flynn very long?"

The cup rattled but Ann's voice was calm. "I live across the hall from him. We don't really know each other that well. Becky fell and hit her head yesterday and Flynn knew that I was a doctor so he came and got me."

"A doctor. I didn't know that. So you don't know Flynn all that well. I'm surprised. The two of you seem quite comfortable with each other."

"Comfortable? I'm not sure that word applies to Flynn." She realized that her comment might sound like a criticism because she continued hurriedly. "I mean, he just doesn't seem the type—"

Louise laughed. "Don't worry. I know just what you mean. And you're right. The word comfortable and Flynn don't really go together. Now Mark was a different story. He was so easy to get along with. Flynn was always too restless and full of questions. I think that's why he and his father have always had a hard time getting along.

"Mark was a strong boy but he was willing to bend in the direction his father wanted. Flynn is just too much like his father. Neither of them knows how to bend. It's a shame. They have so much to give each other. Flynn especially has so much to give to those he cares about."

She didn't lift her head from her needlepoint. Ann could either take the point or not as she chose. Louise had seen the way Flynn looked at Ann and her maternal instincts were telling her that Ann could be exactly what her son needed in his life. She didn't want to be a pushy parent, but it wouldn't hurt to nudge just a little.

Chapter Five

If Ann had seriously believed that her involvement
with Becky and Flynn was going to end after the visit
to his parents, she was doomed to disappointment.
Over the next few days, the focus of her life seemed to
shift.

Ever since graduating from medical school, her life
had centered on her work and, before that, it had
centered on school. When she took a vacation, she
used the time to catch up on medical journals; her
visits with her father were spent discussing ways to
advance her career.

When she'd thought ahead, she'd never really considered whether or not things were always going to be
that way. She'd never given much thought to a husband or children. There'd never been any room to
think about them. Somewhere in the back of her mind
were the usual dreams of a home and family, but
they'd never been given any room to grow and solid-
ify and they'd remained vague, nebulous images
without real focus.

Now, in the space of a few hours, her life had been
turned upside down. Whether she wished it or not, she
was caught up in Becky's life. Through her, Ann was

caught up in Flynn McCallister's life. It wasn't that either Flynn or Becky asked her to spend her free time with them. There just didn't seem to be anything else to do.

The morning after the visit to Flynn's parents, she woke up and told herself that she was not going to go across the hall. This was her day off and she had things to do. Things that didn't include a little girl and a dangerously attractive man.

"Not that *I'm* attracted to him, of course." Oscar stirred and raised his head to blink at her. Ann stared at him in the mirror, aware that she was taking a great deal of time with her makeup, considering that she was planning on relaxing at home. "One kiss is nothing these days. It was a pleasant kiss but no big deal. Flynn McCallister is a playboy. Maybe he's got a heart of gold when it comes to children but he's still a playboy. The man doesn't have a job!"

Oscar yawned. "I may just go over to make sure that Becky is doing all right but then I'm going to come right back here and catch up on my reading. Besides, Flynn probably hasn't been up this early since he was in high school. It might be amusing to see how he's coping with a child in the house."

Oscar yawned again and put his head back down. He knew an excuse when he heard one.

AS A MATTER OF FACT, Flynn was coping quite well. Self-preservation had led him to get up early and make his own coffee before Becky could bring him some of her deadly brew. When the doorbell rang, he was showered, shaved and fixing breakfast for himself and Becky. Becky was drawing pictures at the table.

"Answer the door, would you, honey?"

"Sure, Mr. Flynn. Should I tell them that we don't want to buy anything?"

"I doubt if it's a salesman. Not if Joe's doing his job."

"Who's Joe?"

"Joe is the man downstairs who's paid to tell salesmen to go away."

"Gee, that sounds like an easy job."

She hopped off her chair and trotted out of the kitchen while Flynn was turning the bacon. He knew it was Ann even before he heard her voice. After all, who else could it be? Everyone else had to ring through from downstairs.

Though his back was to the door, he knew the moment she stepped into the room. It was amazing to think that they'd lived across the hall from each other for two years. Two years and he'd only kissed her yesterday. He'd had his fantasies about his uptight, disapproving neighbor, but none of them had come close to the reality of the way she'd felt in his arms.

He set down the fork and turned to look at her, letting his eyes skim over the emerald-striped top and white pants to settle on the deep red of her hair. He could still remember the feel of it against his hands, and he wanted to cross the room and pull the pins out and let it spill through his fingers.

"Good morning."

Ann felt herself flushing under the look in his eyes, though she couldn't quite put her finger on why. He didn't leer, he didn't ogle, but he made her feel intensely aware of her femininity in a way that was really rather pleasant.

"Good morning. I didn't mean to interrupt your breakfast."

"That's okay. Have a seat and I'll stir up a couple more eggs and you can join us."

Ann protested politely. She never ate breakfast. She detested greasy bacon and equally greasy eggs. The fat and cholesterol content of the average American breakfast was enough to give a person instantly hard arteries. If she ate anything at all, it was a cup of yogurt with a few fresh berries.

"I'm really not hungry."

"There's always room for bacon."

Ten minutes later, she found herself sitting down to a breakfast of bacon, eggs, potatoes and toast and enjoying every bite. Becky ate with the healthy appetite of a growing child, and Ann found her enjoyment of the meal tangled with her enjoyment of the company.

Flynn pushed his plate away and poured himself a second cup of coffee. Ann thought about pointing out the hazards of caffeine and then decided that it was none of her concern. Besides, he didn't look as if caffeine had done any damage to his nerves so far. If anyone had ever been the personification of a laid-back Californian, it was Flynn McCallister.

"Becky and I are going shopping today. Her wardrobe needs updating. Want to join us?" His tone was casual, as if it didn't matter to him one way or another.

Of course she wasn't going to go. She had other things to do with her time. But Becky did need clothing, and could a man—a bachelor—really be trusted to buy suitable clothes for a little girl? Still, it wasn't her problem. The mental argument took only a few seconds and was still waging when she heard herself say, "Sure, I would love to go shopping with you."

Shopping with a man and a little girl was a different experience for Ann. She was a very organized shopper. When she went to a store, she had a specific need in mind and she purchased exactly that need or she bought nothing at all. The only exception to this rule was shoes. She couldn't resist shoes and she had several pairs that she'd probably never find an occasion to wear.

Flynn, on the other hand, didn't try to resist anything. Rather than going to an exclusive children's store and asking a buyer to help them choose a wardrobe for Becky, they drove to a nearby mall. On a Monday afternoon, the stores were reasonably free of crowds, but Ann wasn't sure that this was an advantage. Maybe crowds would have curbed some of Flynn's enthusiasm. As it was, there was nothing to deter him as they swept through the stores, much like Sherman marching through Georgia. Instead of leaving fire and destruction in their wake, they left charge slips and checks. In return, they received promises of immediate delivery.

By the time Ann managed to convince him that Becky had a wardrobe any little girl would kill for, Flynn had thought of toys. Ann shuddered as they invaded the toy store. Within minutes, she'd lost her companions in the high-walled aisles, and she retreated to a bench in the mall to rest her feet and hope that Flynn would remember that Becky would probably prefer a doll to a race car. She needn't have worried. He bought both.

It took Becky and Flynn an hour to come out, loaded down with packages. Clothes could be trusted to be delivered, but toys were another matter altogether. It was hard to tell who was more excited. The last of Becky's reticence had vanished beneath the excitement of being able to buy just what she wanted, and she chattered happily about the Barbie doll Mr. Flynn had bought her, complete with a wardrobe.

"Shoes and everything, Ann." They were on their way to the car to leave off the packages, and Becky's childish voice echoed in the cavernous parking structure. In her excitement at describing every detail of every small garment, Becky slid her hand into Ann's, skipping happily. Ann was unprepared for the rush of feeling the simple gesture brought.

Becky's hand felt so small, so vulnerable. Looking down, Ann was struck by the absolute trust Becky had given to her and to Flynn. She had literally put her life in their hands. Her work at the hospital occasionally took her to the children's ward, and she'd always been awed by the confidence a sick child had in the doctors and nurses who treated them. They didn't question, didn't doubt, they simply accepted that the adults were there to help them.

Becky was doing much the same. She wasn't ill but she was vulnerable, and she was trusting that Ann and Flynn would take care of her, find her mother and put her life back together again. Ann's fingers tightened slightly over the little girl's. She was as committed to Becky's needs as Flynn was, whether she liked it or not.

"...red with black stripes and Mr. Flynn says it will go just like a real one." Ann shook off her preoccupation in time to hear Becky's last words. They had stopped next to Flynn's Mercedes and Flynn had opened the trunk.

"Flynn bought you a toy car?"

"It's not a toy, it's a working rep...reptile."

"He bought you a snake?"

"Becky means a replica." Flynn took the packages that Becky had handed to Ann, his eyes not meeting hers. "Let's go get something to eat. Are you hungry, Becky?" If he'd hoped to distract her with the offer of food, he was disappointed.

"Sure. I'm starved. The car isn't for me, Ann. Mr. Flynn bought it for hisself."

"Himself." Ann made the correction automatically, her eyes on Flynn's back as he shut the Mercedes's trunk a little more forcefully than was necessary. "So you bought a toy car."

Flynn turned to look at her, his brows raised, as if amazed that she would question such a thing. It was difficult to be sure in the dim light of the parking garage, but Ann was almost positive that his face was flushed. Flynn McCallister? Blushing? What an incredible idea.

"It's a remote controlled replica of a Jaguar XKE."

"That's different than a toy?" Ann took Becky's hand as they turned to go back into the mall. Flynn took Becky's other hand as she skipped between them, oblivious to the byplay going on between the two adults.

"It's a sophisticated piece of engineering."

"But not a toy?"

"It's a very educational piece of equipment. It teaches good eye-hand coordination." Ann didn't say anything. The look she gave him over Becky's head said it all. Flynn threw her an exasperated glance.

"They didn't make them when I was a kid." He sounded so defensive that Ann had to bite her cheek to keep from laughing out loud.

"Well, I hope it helps your eye-hand coordination."

The look he gave her was all male. "I think my eye-hand coordination is pretty good. I haven't had any complaints so far. I could demonstrate."

Ann felt the color surge into her cheeks at the blatant invitation. She could only hope that the dim light was as kind to her as it had been to him. "I don't think that will be necessary."

"I was afraid you'd say that."

The regret in his eyes was only half joking, and Ann felt a twinge of purely feminine pleasure before she looked away. Flynn's eyes lingered on her a moment longer before dropping to Becky.

"Well, Rebecca Antoinette, what would you like for lunch?"

"Corn dogs and French fries with catsup."

Flynn shuddered, his eyes closing for a moment. "Sounds terrific."

Ann laughed and wondered if it was foolish to be so happy over nothing.

"LOOK AT IT GO, Mr. Flynn. I bet it could go clear to the moon."

"It just might if you don't hold onto the string really tight."

Flynn reached out to steady Becky's small hands on the spool of string and then leaned back on his elbows, staring up at the bright scarlet kite that floated high above them. Since it was a weekday, the park was uncrowded. The weather was perfect. Becky had informed him that there was no temperature at all, and he knew just what she meant. The air felt neither warm nor cool. The sky above was a warm blue, a shade that Los Angeles didn't see very often. The residents had learned to savor it as long as it lasted.

"How high do you think it is, Mr. Flynn? One hundred miles?"

Flynn squinted at the kite. "Not an inch over ninety-nine miles." The kite kicked in the wind, swooping back and forth, weaving dancing patterns against the blue sky.

Flynn closed his eyes for a moment, savoring a feeling of peace like he hadn't known in years. Not since Mark's death had he felt so relaxed. He shifted one hand, touching Becky's slim back affectionately. It felt so right to be here with her. He'd never thought of himself as a family man, but Becky was making him reconsider. And Ann. Ann was making him reconsider a lot of things.

It was hard to believe that they'd spent the last two years across the hall from each other and barely exchanged a civil word. Like Becky, she'd become an integral part of his life. It was hard to imagine a time when she hadn't been there.

Dangerous thinking, McCallister. Next thing you know, you'll be thinking about rings and babies.

And why not?

The thought was so surprising that his eyes flew open and he sat up, oblivious to Becky's startled look. He'd begun to think of himself as a confirmed bachelor. He hadn't thought about marriage and children in years. Now, suddenly, the idea seemed not quite so alien. Appealing almost.

"Something wrong, Mr. Flynn?"

He shook himself and gave Becky a smile. Time enough to consider the implications of his thoughts later. "Not a thing. Come on, let's see if we can get your kite to go even higher."

Becky scrambled to her feet as he stood up, her fingers clenched around the spool. "I don't think it can go higher. It's awful high now."

"If we've got more string, we can get it higher."

She looked from him to the kite scudding across the sky above them. Her expression was cautious, doubtful. "What if it goes so high we lose it?"

"We'll buy another one." He grinned down at her. "Where's your spirit of adventure?" She eyed him cautiously before handing him the spool of string. Flynn took it from her with one hand and reached out to ruffle her hair with the other. "Don't look so worried, urchin."

It was clear that Becky had never learned how to be a proper child. She worried too much. Who better to teach her the fine points of childhood than someone who'd never grown up? He grinned and began to unreel the string, watching the kite dip and sway as it climbed higher.

"Let's see if we can set a world record in kite flying."

"Okay." Becky's eyes were wide as she stared up at the kite, picking up his enthusiasm. "I bet Ann will be impressed when she gets home and we tell her how high we got our kite."

When Ann gets home. Flynn repeated the phrase in his mind. It made the three of them sound like a family. It was rather frightening to realize how right that sounded.

ANN LEANED AGAINST the padded wall of the elevator and closed her eyes. It seemed as if her work schedule was getting more and more hectic. From the moment she arrived at the hospital, one thing after another claimed her attention. She used to tell herself that it was exhilarating, but today it had been near to drudgery. She'd always thought she knew what she wanted out of life. She'd become a doctor, work her way up the staff hierarchy in a good hospital and sometime before she grew too old to hear him, her father would tell her that he was proud of her.

Somehow, since letting Becky and Flynn into her life, her goals seemed skewed. Medicine suddenly didn't seem as interesting or exciting. Becoming chief of staff someday held no interest at all. She shook her head. It was a temporary state. She'd wanted this for too long, wanted to prove herself to her father. Once Becky's mother was found, her life would get back to normal and her future would fall into place again.

Ann tried not to think of how impossible the day had seemed. Her heart hadn't been in the job, and that was a dangerous thing for a doctor. She'd gone through all the motions and done all the right things but, in the back of her mind, she'd wondered what Becky and Flynn were doing. She'd wished she were doing it with them.

She was getting too involved.

But it's only for Becky's sake. As soon as her mother is found, I'll be out of the picture.

But what about Flynn? Are you going to back away from him?

Of course. I'm only seeing him because that's where Becky is. It's nothing to do with him personally.

And if she just kept telling herself that, she might believe it. The mental argument came to a halt with the elevator. She opened her eyes as the door slid open.

Never had the peace and quiet of her own apartment held more appeal. She wouldn't even go over to see Becky tonight. She'd give Flynn a call and make sure that the little girl was all right, ask if there was any progress toward finding her mother and then she'd hang up. That was all anyone could possibly expect of her.

Ann stepped out of the elevator, the decision firm in her mind. And then nearly jumped out of her skin as a small red object hurtled toward her across the smooth carpet. She had only a moment of panic before she recognized it. This must be the infamous sophisticated piece of engineering. The toy car that Flynn had bought the day before.

It came to a halt inches from her feet as if to invite her to admire its shiny red paint. Ann had to admit that it looked remarkably like the real thing. It scooted a little forward and then back, reminding her of a small child shifting from one foot to another, impatient with adult slowness. Then she saw the piece of paper threaded onto the antenna. She bent and slid the paper loose, her fingers hesitant. It would be just her luck to break Flynn's new toy. Nothing broke, however, and she looked at the note, finding her name inscribed in a bold script that had to be Flynn's.

Ann,
Becky and I would love to have your company at dinner. No corn dogs. I promise. Becky wants to show off her new dolls. I just want to show off.
                                        Flynn

The signature was a huge scrawl, as fascinating and unconventional as the man himself. Ann stared at the note and then looked down at the little car. She wasn't going to go, of course. She glanced at Flynn's door, which was open a crack. It didn't take a genius to figure out that he was crouched behind the crack, controlling the car. The image was so silly, so appealing that Ann found herself smiling for the first time all day.

She scrambled in her purse for a pen. Balancing the paper on her purse, she scribbled a reply.

> Am disappointed at the thought of no corn dogs but will try to bear up. Expect me in half an hour. Looking forward to seeing your and Becky's new toys.
>
>   Ann

She threaded the note back onto the antenna and watched as the car made a quick reversing turn and spun for Flynn's door. The door opened just wide enough for the little car to shoot through and then shut, leaving Ann alone.

"So much for being strong-minded and spending a quiet evening at home." But there was no real regret in the muttered words.

Flynn kept his promise. There was not a corn dog in sight when the three of them sat down to dinner. Fried chicken with all the trimmings covered the table to the groaning point. Ann took one look and gave up trying to count the cholesterol content. It was a meal chosen to appeal to a child and yet offer something substantial for an adult.

"This looks fabulous." She could say the words with absolute sincerity. In fact, she couldn't remember the last time a meal had looked quite so good.

Unless it was the breakfast Flynn had prepared the morning before. "You're a wonderful cook, Flynn."

"Thanks. My father thinks it's a wimpy occupation for a man but I enjoy it. I get tired of restaurant food. Becky helped tonight."

"I made the biscuits."

Ann looked at the lumpy, misshapen masses of dough and forced a smile as she took one. It seemed to weigh a great deal in proportion to its size and, when she tried to cut it open to put butter on it, it took quite a bit of hacking and sawing to get it apart. She stared at the grayed dough inside and swallowed hard.

"They look wonderful, Becky." Her eyes met Flynn's, bright blue with amusement.

"Becky believes in kneading all doughs thoroughly."

"Oh." There didn't seem to be anything else to say. "Aren't you having a biscuit, Becky?"

Becky shook her head, her mouth full of chicken. "I don't like biscuits. They always taste like old rocks when Mama makes them."

"I see." She set the biscuits aside, hoping that Becky would forget about it. There was no way she was going to risk thousands of dollars in orthodontic work by attempting to bite into that ominous mass.

"So what did you two do today?"

"We went to the park. It was a great day for flying kites."

"Mr. Flynn got a big kite and we flew it for a long time only then he got it caught in a tree."

"I prefer to think of it as the tree got in my way."

Ann answered his grin with a smile, surprised to realize how right it felt to be sitting across the table from him. She pushed the thought away. She didn't want to look too closely at where her relationship with Flynn was heading. For once in her life, she didn't want to look at the future. She just wanted to enjoy the present.

After dinner, Ann loaded the dishwasher with only a few token protests from Flynn. She insisted that it was the least she could do, and he didn't argue long. She was afraid to run the biscuits down the disposal. They looked far more deadly than the chicken bones, so she threw them in the trash, burying them deep in the hope that Becky would never find them.

She wandered out into the living room to find Flynn and Becky sitting on the sofa, their attention on a box on the table in front of them. Or at least Becky's attention was on the box. Flynn's attention was on nothing in particular unless Becky was talking to him. Ann crossed the soft carpet and sank onto the sofa on Becky's other side.

"What have you got?"

"Pictures." The succinct answer came from Becky. Flynn appeared to be half dozing.

Ann reached for a handful of the photographs that were scattered across the table. She expected to find family pictures, and she admitted to a mild curiosity to see what Flynn had looked like as a child. But the photos she held weren't your typical family shots.

The first was a picture of the park across the street. A light drizzle gave the background a gray look that could have been depressing. But the focus of the shot wasn't the weather. It was a little boy wearing a bright red raincoat and hat with incongruously bare feet. The camera had caught him in the act of jumping into a shallow puddle, his face ecstatic with anticipation.

Leaning drunkenly against a bench nearby was a pair of red rain boots.

The picture made her smile, but it brought back the feeling of being a child—the intensity with which children lived every minute of every day.

The next photo was of an old woman. Ann assumed it was downtown Los Angeles, but it could have been any city. The woman's clothes were ragged but clean. Her face was weathered with decades of hard living, but there was pride in the set of her chin, in the clarity of her eyes. Pride that wasn't dimmed by the shopping cart of belongings that sat next to her. Her gray hair was pulled back into a bun, and stuck in the thin strands was a bright red carnation, its jaunty color a defiant denial of the circumstances.

Ann blinked back tears and moved to the next picture. Each photo touched the emotions, some happy, some sad, but all of them evocative. They spoke to the heart, more than the mind.

She had no idea how long she'd been looking at them when she looked up. Becky had disappeared and Ann could hear her somewhere behind the sofa, talking to her dolls. Flynn was sitting just where he had been, his long body relaxed back into the deep cushions, only his watchful eyes telling her that he was still awake.

"Did you take these?"

"It's a hobby."

"They're beautiful."

"Thanks. I've got a small darkroom and I enjoy playing with it."

"You've done a lot more than play with these. They're full of emotion. Have you had much published?"

He laughed and leaned forward to gather up the photos scattered on the table, laying them back in the box. "I've never submitted them."

"Never submitted?" Ann looked at him as if he'd just confessed to murder. "How could you not submit them?"

He cocked an eyebrow at her appalled expression. "It's a hobby."

"But they're so good."

"It's still a hobby. Everything in life doesn't have to have a goal, you know."

No, she didn't know. He could see that the very concept was foreign to her. She sat there staring at him as if he were an alien from Venus. There she was on his sofa, her hair pulled back in the inevitable chignon, her green eyes wide with confusion, her chin set with what he suspected was a determination to argue with him. All he wanted to do was pull her across the few feet that separated them and kiss her senseless.

He sighed inaudibly. This was a hell of a time to discover a lust for his uptight neighbor. With Becky playing only a few feet away and Ann ready to chastise him for his worthless life-style, it was unlikely that she'd be receptive to what he really wanted to suggest. But it never hurt to dream.

"These photographs are good, Flynn. Really good. I know you could get them published."

He took the pictures she still held and put them in the box with the others. "I probably could. But I don't want to."

"Why not?"

"Ann, if I sold some photos, it would cease to be a hobby and become a career. I couldn't play with it anymore. People would expect me to take wonderful photos according to their schedules. It wouldn't be fun anymore.''

"But you can't just take pictures like that and not do something with them."

"Why not?"

The simple question seemed to stymie her. She stared at him blankly for a moment. "You just can't."

Flynn sought for another way to explain it to her. "How would you feel if one of your hobbies suddenly became a job?"

"I don't know. I don't have a hobby."

It was his turn to stare at her in stunned silence. "You don't have a hobby? Everybody has a hobby. Do you sew? Crochet? Knit? Paint? Grow African violets?" Ann shook her head in answer to every suggestion and his suggestions became more outrageous. Becky came to lean on the back of the sofa and threw in a few suggestions of her own.

"I've got it. You're a closet taxidermist."

Helpless with laughter, Ann shook her head.

"What's a taxi... taxipermist?" Becky's question came out on a yawn, making Flynn realize how late it was.

He stood up, abandoning the subject of Ann's hobbies for the moment. "It's someone who gives permanents to taxi drivers. Time for bed, urchin." He ignored the inevitable protests and herded her toward the bathroom with instructions to wash her hands.

"I'll supervise." Ann followed Becky into the bathroom and he could hear the two of them talking. He turned down the sheets on Becky's bed and then looked around the room. It was funny how just a few nights with Becky sleeping here and already the room felt lived in again. Mark's presence was fading to pleasant memories.

He turned as Becky and Ann entered the room. Becky was tucked into bed with Frankie the giraffe snuggled beside her.

"Tell me a story, Mr. Flynn." Flynn told her a story about a frog who became a prince and the princess who loved him even when he was a frog. Behind him, he could hear Ann moving around, quietly putting away the last of the day's purchases. It felt so right. It felt like . . . home.

He finished the story and reached up to tuck the covers under Becky's chin. "Good night, Becky."

"Mr. Flynn? Do you think I'll ever see my mama again?"

Flynn was aware of Ann coming to stand behind him, but he knew the question was his to field. What was he supposed to say? Life didn't offer any guarantees. Not even to children.

"We've got a man looking for her, honey. He's very good at finding people. All we can do is cross our fingers that he'll find her soon."

"What's goin' to happen to me if he don't find her?"

Flynn brushed the ragged bangs off her forehead, telling himself not to promise too much. Behind him, he could feel Ann's tension. He looked at Becky, seeing the uncertainty in her eyes, the hint of a quiver that shook her stubborn chin and the absolute trust she gave him. And suddenly the answer was very simple.

"I'll take care of you, Becky. Whatever happens, I'll take care of you."

The uncertainty faded from her eyes. If Flynn said he'd take care of her, she believed him. She yawned. "What are we gonna do tomorrow?"

"Tomorrow, you and I are going to find a hobby for Ann."

"That'll be fun."

"I think so. Now, go to sleep." He dropped a kiss on her forehead and then waited while Ann did the same. They left the room, leaving the door partially open behind them.

"That's an awfully big promise." Ann's voice was carefully noncritical.

Flynn ran his fingers through his hair. "I know, but what else could I say to her? Besides, I meant it."

"I'm sure the detective will find Becky's mother."

"I hope so. But whatever happens, I'm going to make sure Becky doesn't suffer for it."

Ann reached out to touch the back of his hand. "I know you will."

ANN DIDN'T GIVE any more thought to Flynn's threat to find her a hobby. She knew he was just kidding. After all, nobody could choose a hobby for another person. She might have known that this was another rule that Flynn McCallister had never heard of.

The next evening when she got home, she didn't even bother to pretend to herself that she wasn't going to go to Flynn's apartment. Like it or not, she was involved. As long as he had Becky, Ann was involved in his life.

She changed clothes and fed Oscar, giving him some extra attention to make up for the fact that she was leaving him alone again. An hour after arriving home, she was knocking on Flynn's door. Becky answered the door.

"Ann! Mr. Flynn is making tacos. He says there's lots if you want to eat with us." Becky took Ann's hand and pulled her into the apartment. Ann was surprised by how much it felt like coming home. "We got you a hobby."

"You did what?"

Flynn came to the kitchen doorway in time to hear her exclamation. He gave her his most devilish grin. "Ann! How nice to see you. Becky, why don't you go get Ann's hobby. I'm sure she must be wild with excitement. Are you going to be joining us for dinner?"

"That depends." She checked to make sure that Becky was out of earshot and lowered her voice to be safe. "Did Becky cook any of it?"

Flynn's grin widened. "She made the instant pudding for dessert."

"Then maybe I'll join you for dinner."

Becky ran back into the room, a gaily wrapped package in her hands. She was a far cry from the ragged little girl Ann had met less than a week ago. Her hot pink cotton play pants and matching T-shirt gave color to her rather pale face. Her hair still needed a good cut, but Flynn had pulled it back from her face and clipped it into two pink barrettes. She looked like a normal, healthy child.

"Here." She thrust the package into Ann's hands, her face glowing with excitement. "Mr. Flynn and I picked it out together."

"Bring it into the kitchen so I can keep an eye on the tacos." Ann and Becky followed Flynn into the kitchen, and Ann couldn't help but sniff appreciatively at the spicy aromas that filled the room.

She set the package down on the table and tugged off the ribbon. Becky stood beside her, hopping back and forth with excitement. "Do you need help getting it open?"

It was clear that Ann's usual methodical procedure was not going to do. She nodded and Becky's small fingers made short shrift of the wrapping paper. When the contents were revealed, Ann didn't know what to say. Lying in the tattered remnants of the wrapping was a paint-by-numbers kit. A picture of a bowl of flowers.

She looked at Flynn who looked back at her with a totally bland expression. "Becky and I thought you'd enjoy it."

"It's wonderful. Thank you." She hoped the comment sounded enthusiastic enough for Becky. She didn't worry about Flynn. After all, he had clearly bought it as a joke. He didn't really expect her to do anything with it. Paint-by-numbers. How silly could you get?

She could never quite explain to herself how it happened. She took the kit home, planning to throw it away, but it seemed a shame to throw it out without at least opening it. And then those little pots of paint looked kind of interesting. It couldn't hurt to dab a few colors on the canvas. And before she knew it, it was midnight and she was still hunched over the table, dabbing little bits of paint into numbered segments on the picture.

And damned if she wasn't having a thoroughly good time!

Chapter Six

"I'm sorry, Mr. McCallister. I wish I had more news for you. We'll keep looking but, frankly, we're beginning to run out of directions to go."

Flynn nodded, his eyes on the rather bilious floral print that hung over Leon Devoe's desk. Leon Devoe fit neither his name nor his profession. Everyone knew that private investigators were either tall and stunningly handsome with a slightly world-weary attitude, or short and slimy and out to cheat every client who came within reach. Leon looked like an ad for Mr. Average. Average size, average looks, average honesty. But he came with high recommendations.

"Perhaps if I could talk to the little girl. She might be able to tell me something that would help me to locate her mother."

"No." Flynn shook his head. "I don't want to involve Becky any more than we have to. She's scared enough without having someone asking questions. I've told you everything she knows about her mother's disappearance."

Leon shrugged and shuffled the papers on his desk. "I don't suppose it would do much good anyway. Frankly, there are a number of odd things about this woman. I can't find any record of her or the child past about three years ago. It's as if they fell out of the sky and into Los Angeles."

"That might have been about the time that Becky's father took off. She's a little vague on the dates."

"Well, if her mother wanted to hide the two of them from the child's father, she did a remarkably good job of it. I'm sure I'll be able to trace them but it could take quite some time."

Flynn leaned forward in his chair. "I'm not all that interested in their past. I want to know where the woman is now. I want to know why she didn't show up when she was supposed to."

"I understand, Mr. McCallister, but as I told you, we're running into walls. Beyond the fact that she left with a man, just as the little girl said, we haven't been able to find out much more. No one remembers the car, except that it was brown or possibly tan or maybe black. No one remembers the man except that he was tall or possibly short and he might have had brown hair, though one of the neighbors distinctly remembers that his hair was red."

Flynn stood up, his movements tight with controlled impatience. "Didn't anyone pay any attention at all?"

"Not really. Apparently, it wasn't at all unusual to see the woman leaving with a man. It was a normal occurrence. There was no reason for anyone to take special note of the child's mother going off for a weekend trip."

"Except that she didn't come back from this trip."

"Exactly. But there was no way of knowing that ahead of time."

"Have you managed to find out anything at all that might tell us where she went?"

Leon shook his head slowly. "I wish I could say otherwise, but so far we've found very little of any use."

"Let me know if anything changes. You've got my number."

Leon stood up, coming around the desk to open the door for Flynn. "Rest assured, Mr. McCallister, that you will be the first to know if we find out anything helpful. But, frankly, I can't hold out much hope."

The two men shook hands and Flynn stepped out into the hall, listening to the door shut behind him. He didn't move away immediately. He wasn't looking forward to going home and telling Ann that he hadn't found out anything at all. As time passed, it was beginning to look less and less likely that Becky's mother was coming back. How was he supposed to tell a little girl that her mother might never return?

CHILD AND CAT STARED at each other with equal intensity. Each waiting for the other to make a move. Oscar's paw darted out, catching hold of the old sock and jerking it from Becky's hand. With a triumphant lunge, he was off and running, Becky hot on his trail.

Ann looked up from the medical journal she was reading and smiled. She'd been concerned about introducing Becky and Oscar, uncertain of how the big tomcat would take to having his territory invaded by a small human. After some initial caution, Oscar had apparently decided that Becky had been imported solely for his pleasure. When he was tired of playing, Becky was content to sit beside him and pet him. Oscar was in cat heaven.

Ann looked at the clock and frowned. It was only five minutes since the last time she'd looked at the clock. This was ridiculous. Flynn would return as soon as he could. He'd only been gone a little over an hour. As soon as he'd talked to the private detective and found out if there were any leads to Becky's mother, he'd come home. There was no sense in watching the clock.

When the doorbell rang fifteen minutes later, Ann practically flew to the door, Becky hard on her heels. Oscar watched them from a safe perch on the sofa. Ann flung open the door, hoping that she'd be able to read something from his expression. They'd already agreed not to tell Becky where he'd been, so until they could get Becky out of the room, they wouldn't be able to talk openly. But surely he'd find a way to let her know if there was any news.

"Flynn—"

"Mr. Flynn—"

Both sentences came to an abrupt halt. The man standing outside the door was definitely not Flynn. He was short, stocky and balding, and the expression on his face bore no resemblance to Flynn's lazy charm. His eyes traveled from Ann's face to Becky.

"Dad." Ann knew her tone fell short of enthusiasm and she repeated the word, trying to sound less like she'd just discovered an encyclopedia salesman on her doorstep. "Dad."

"Ann." He nodded. "Obviously, you were expecting someone else."

"That's okay. Obviously, you aren't someone else." He didn't bother to smile at her weak attempt at humor.

"May I come in?"

"Of course. I'm sorry. I didn't mean to keep you standing there." She stepped back, aware of Becky retreating to stand next to Oscar. She shut the door behind her father and followed him into the living room. "Dad, this is Rebecca Sinclair. She's staying across the hall and I'm taking care of her for a little while. Becky, this is my father, Mr. Perry."

He acknowledged the introduction with a short nod. "Staying with the McCallister fellow, is she? I thought you were steering clear of him."

Robert Perry believed that children should be seen and not heard. He also believed that they should be treated as if they were part of the furniture, which included not only silence, but deafness.

Luckily, the doorbell rang again before Ann had to find an answer for her father's comment. Her pace was much more subdued this time, and she waited until the door was fully open before greeting her visitor.

"Flynn." They had only an instant in the semi-privacy of the hall. There was no time for Ann to ask any questions about his visit with the private detective. Her eyes met his and he shook his head slightly, the only thing they had time for before Becky clutched Flynn around the knees.

"Hi, urchin." He bent and scooped her up, holding her casually under one arm. Her giggles drew a smile from Ann, a smile that died when she looked at her father.

"Flynn, this is my father, Robert Perry. Dad, this is Flynn McCallister."

The two men nodded. Robert Perry's face expressed his disapproval of both Flynn and Becky. "I understand Ann has been baby-sitting for you."

"I suppose you could call it that."

"My daughter is a very busy woman. I hope you don't plan to intrude on her time like this again."

"Dad!" Ann could feel the color coming up in her cheeks. She looked at Flynn, half-expecting him to stalk out in a rage. But, of course, Flynn McCallister never did the expected thing.

One black brow arched upward, and his mouth twisted in a half smile that brought an angry flush to Robert Perry's face even before Flynn spoke.

"I think Ann can take care of herself. She's never hesitated to speak her mind in the past. Of course, you have to be willing to listen to hear what she's saying." His words fell into a little pool of silence. Ann held her breath, waiting for the explosion.

Flynn seemed oblivious to the tension. He shifted Becky from one arm to the other, holding her against his hip as if she weighed nothing. "Ann, we're having chili dogs tonight if you want to join us."

He turned and left without another word to her father, tugging the door shut behind him, cutting off the sound of Becky's giggling pleas to be put down. Ann stared at the door for a long moment, surprised by the strength of the urge to follow him.

She had to force herself to look at her father, pinning a determinedly cheerful expression on her face. Maybe he would just ignore Flynn's comments. One look at his purple complexion told her that he wasn't going to ignore anything. It was going to be a rough visit.

"HAVE A GLASS of wine."

Ann shook her head. "I really shouldn't stay. It's

late and . . . thank you." She took the glass he handed her and sipped the pale red contents.

"You'll sleep better after a nice glass of *pinot noir*."

Flynn sank into a chair at right angles to the sofa and propped his stockinged feet on the glass coffee table. He looked absolutely boneless, slouched in the chair, a wineglass in one hand, the other hand relaxed on the wide arm of the chair. He had nice hands, long fingers and neatly clipped nails. Artistic hands.

Ann took another sip of wine and felt some of the tension seep out. She slid farther back on the sofa and leaned her head against its back. It was so peaceful here. Becky was asleep; the city was quiet beneath them. No one was demanding anything of her. How had it happened that, in the space of a few short days, Flynn McCallister had gone from being a thorn in her side to being an oasis of calm?

Of course, it was only temporary. As soon as Becky's mother was found, she and Flynn would go their separate ways again. Not that they'd go back to being antagonists, but they'd certainly have no reason to do more than nod politely in the hall. Why wasn't that thought more reassuring?

"What did the private investigator have to say about Becky's mother? Any luck?"

Flynn shook his head. "Not much. He's found out quite a bit about her but nothing that tells us where she might have disappeared to." He swirled the wine in his glass, his expression uncharacteristically serious. "She doesn't sound like your average mother who belongs to the PTA and bakes cookies every second Tuesday."

"So? Most women don't fit that pattern anymore."

"True. But most women don't have a different boyfriend every weekend and no visible means of support."

"You think she's a . . ." Ann cleared her throat, her eyes going toward the room where Becky was asleep.

"I don't know." Flynn took another swallow of his wine, his frown deepening. "She must love Becky or she wouldn't have bothered to keep her. Maybe she is earning her living in the oldest profession. Maybe she doesn't have a choice."

"Still, that's not going to be very good for Becky, especially when she gets old enough to understand what's going on."

"It would explain why her mother has instilled a fear of the 'welfare people' in Becky. I imagine they would take her away if her mother's doing what I think she's doing."

"What are we going to tell Becky?" She used the plural without thought. It was no longer possible to pretend that she wasn't involved in this situation.

"Nothing. At least not until we have some news of her mother. She's happy here. I'm just going to let her stay that way."

"What if her mother's never found?"

Flynn downed the last of his wine and stared broodingly at the glass. "We'll cross that bridge when it gets here."

Ann took another swallow of wine, feeling the warm glow of it settle in her stomach and then ease its way through her body.

"Did Becky get to sleep all right?"

"No problem. I told her a story and she went out like a light before I even got to the punch line. She asked where you were."

Ann tried to ignore the pleasure the words gave her. She was getting too emotionally involved here. She was going to get hurt. "What did you tell her?"

"I told her that you'd asked me to give her a kiss for you and that you'd see her tomorrow."

"That was nice."

"I thought so. Of course, you owe me a kiss now." Ann's eyes flew to his face. He gave her a lazy smile that set up a fluttering in her stomach. "I'll collect later."

"Oh. Fine." Fine? Had she really said fine? It had to be the wine. Maybe he'd drugged it.

"How did the visit with your father go?"

In her current relaxed state, not even the mention of her father could seriously dim the warm glow Ann felt. He seemed so far away.

"The same as usual. I'm not doing well enough. I should be further along in my career. I don't attend the right gatherings. He doesn't like my cat, my apartment, my life-style."

"And he most especially doesn't like Becky and me."

It had to be the wine. She wasn't even upset that he'd hit the nail on the head with such unerring precision.

"It's nothing personal. He just worries that I'll let things get in the way of my career."

"Things like personal relationships?" The question was unanswerable, but he didn't seem to expect a reply. He leaned forward and picked up the wine bottle, filling his own glass before leaning forward to fill Ann's.

"I really shouldn't. It's late."

"You've got to try it now that it's had time to breathe."

She sipped obediently. It didn't taste any different to her, but she nodded and made an appreciative noise. She really should go home, but the sofa felt so wonderfully soft.

"You know, I've found that you can't always fulfill your parents' dreams for you. Sometimes, you just have to do what *you* want to do, even if it disappoints the people you love."

"I *am* doing what I want to do."

"Then you've got nothing to worry about."

Ann frowned into her glass. "It's not that my father isn't proud of me. It's just that he has very high standards. He wanted a boy, you know."

"Well, I, for one, am glad he didn't get what he wanted. You're much too beautiful to make a good boy." He raised his glass in a toast and Ann felt that disturbing tingle of pleasure again.

"Thank you. I don't think that's any consolation to my father."

"I wasn't trying to console him."

"You know, I wish I was more like you." Ann was almost as surprised by her words as he was. Amazing what a couple of glasses of wine could do.

"Like me? I wouldn't have guessed that you harbored a secret desire to be a worthless playboy, as my father so succinctly puts it."

"No, I don't mean that. I mean, I wish I didn't care so much what other people thought. You just go through life doing what you want to do. You don't let what your father wants control your life.''

Flynn's mouth twisted ironically. "Oh, I don't know. In some ways, I am what I am just to spite my father. Nobody is completely free of their parents' influence. You've just got to keep it in perspective.''

"Perspective." Ann yawned. "Did you know that I wanted to be a veterinarian when I was a kid?''

"Why didn't you?''

She swallowed the last of her wine and set the glass down with a thump. "My father thought it was dumb. Doctoring people is more important than animals.'' She yawned again. "I'm sorry. I should have warned you that wine makes me sleepy.''

"That's okay. Do you ever regret it?''

"That wine makes me sleepy? It doesn't cause me much trouble.'' She blinked at him owlishly.

He smiled, his eyes bright with amusement. "Do you ever regret becoming a people doctor instead of an animal doctor?''

"Of course not. People doctoring is much more important.'' Her eyelids felt so heavy. "I really should be going home.''

Flynn watched as her head slipped slowly to the side, her eyes shut, her mouth the slightest bit open as she slid into sleep. There was a funny ache in his chest. She looked so vulnerable. He set his glass down and stood up. He should probably wake her up and send her home. She wasn't going to be happy about falling asleep in front of him. It was too big a chink in the wall she kept between them. He looked at her a moment longer and then left the room.

When he returned, he was carrying a pillow and a blanket. Ann didn't twitch when he tucked the pillow under her head, easing her down to lie on the sofa. He lifted her feet up, slipping her shoes off.

He covered her with the blanket, and she cuddled under its light warmth, snuggling her face into the pillow. Her hair was still pulled back in a loose bun, but a few rebellious strands had escaped the pins to curl around her face. He brushed them back, letting the soft warmth curl around his fingers.

He wasn't entirely sure what was happening between them, but he knew it was a lot more than just concern for Becky. Thirty-three was a hell of a time to fall in love for the first time. He'd almost begun to think it would never happen. He tucked the blanket more firmly around her shoulders and moved away, scooping up the glasses and the half-empty wine bottle on his way to the kitchen.

THE JANGLE OF THE PHONE was an unexpected intrusion and Ann jumped, splashing red paint onto a portion of the picture that was designated for blue.

"Drat!" She dabbed at the errant paint and succeeded in smearing it a little farther. The phone rang again, and she dropped the rag and got up. She hesitated, staring at the phone indecisively. What if it was Flynn? In the two days since she'd awakened on his sofa, she'd managed to avoid much contact with him. She saw him only when Becky was present to act as a buffer. A buffer from what, Ann couldn't have said. All she knew was that Flynn threatened her carefully planned life-style. The wine had made the evening a little fuzzy around the edges, but it hadn't blocked out what had been said.

What had gotten into her that she'd said such things to him? She never talked to anyone like that. Not even to herself. There was something about him that made it all too easy to reveal things she didn't want revealed, say things she didn't even want to think.

The phone rang again, and she took a deep breath and reached for it. It wasn't likely to be Flynn and, even if it was, there was certainly nothing to be afraid of. Maybe he was calling to suggest that they leave for their picnic early.

"Hello?"

"Ann?"

"Oh, hello, Dad." The relief was only temporary. Her father hadn't been entirely happy with her when he left two days ago.

"I wanted to let you know that I've taken matters into my own hands."

"What matters?"

"When we talked about that child that McCallister is keeping, I told you that the only thing to do was call the Social Services. After giving it careful thought, I felt it would be best for all concerned if someone did the right thing so I called Social Services this morning and explained the situation to them."

"You did what?" Ann hadn't thought it was possible to be so angry so quickly. Her voice came out on a breathy note. She was surprised she could get it past the tightness in her throat.

"I know you'll agree that this is the best solution. McCallister is clearly unfit to be taking care of a child and—"

"How dare you?"

"What?"

"How dare you interfere like this?"

"There's no need to get hysterical, Ann."

"I'm not hysterical. I'm mad! Damn it! You had no right!" She slammed the receiver down in the midst of his angry protests about her tone. She stared at the wall for several long seconds, taking deep breaths, suppressing the desire to scream with rage.

Flynn. She had to warn Flynn. Barefoot, paint on her fingers, she flew out of the apartment and across the hall. She knocked, hurting her knuckles with the force she put into the simple gesture. It seemed like hours before the door began to open.

"Flynn, I'm so sorry. My father called—"

"Come in and meet Ms. Davis, Ann. She's here about Becky."

Ann dragged her eyes from the rage that glittered in his and looked past his shoulder to the woman who sat in the living room.

Flynn took her arm and pulled her into the hall, shutting the door behind her with a snap. Ann stretched her stiff facial muscles into a smile and hoped she didn't look as sick as she felt.

"YOU HAVE TO UNDERSTAND, Mr. McCallister, this is a very unusual situation. If you'd reported Rebecca to us when you first found her, she would have been placed in appropriate foster care until her mother was found. Now, the child has had a chance to form an attachment to you. And, of course to you also, Ms. Perry. It will make it much harder for her to settle somewhere else."

Flynn gave the woman a coaxing smile. "Then why move her? You can see that she's doing just fine here. Why not let her stay until her mother is found? I realize that I'm not, perhaps, a typical foster parent but

I've done a pretty good job so far. Becky is happy here. Ann keeps an eye on her health and well-being."

"I tell you what. I can't promise anything but I'll see what I can do to allow you to keep Rebecca." She held up her hand to forestall Flynn's thanks. "It will only be temporary. If her mother isn't found soon, more permanent arrangements will have to be made."

Jane Davis got up, gathering up her briefcase and purse. Flynn and Ann rose with her, both of them smiling with relief. She held out her hand. "I'll call as soon as I've talked to my superiors."

Flynn took her hand, but instead of the expected handshake, he raised it to his lips, kissing her fingers with a courtliness that brought a flutter even to a heart toughened by years of social work.

The door shut and Ann turned to Flynn, wanting to offer some explanation, some apology, some excuse for her father's behavior. Before she could speak, Becky's voice interrupted.

"Is she gone?" The adults turned to find her peering into the living room, her eyes wide and uncertain.

"She's gone."

"She's not going to make me go away with her?"

"Nobody is going to make you go anywhere." Flynn bent to catch the little girl as she flew across the room to him. He swept her up easily, accepting her arms around his neck and returning the hug. Ann swallowed a lump in her throat.

"She wanted to take me away, didn't she?" Becky's voice was muffled by Flynn's shoulder.

"She wanted to make sure that you were all right."

"Is she going to let me stay with you?"

Flynn stroked the back of her head, offering her physical reassurance as well as verbal. "She's going to let you stay with me. She was just worried about you and she wanted to make sure Ann and I were taking good care of you."

Becky snuggled her head deeper into his neck. "What about Mama? Are they going to take me away from Mama?"

Flynn's eyes met Ann's in helpless question. His answer was very carefully phrased. "I'm sure they'll want to talk to your mom when we find her but when they see how much she loves you, everything will be all right."

Apparently that was all the reassurance Becky required. If Mr. Flynn said it was going to be fine, she'd believe him. Her arms loosened around his neck, her world set right again.

Flynn set Becky down and pointed her in the direction of the bedroom. "Go get a jacket and I'll get the picnic." She skipped off, confident that all was right with her world as long as Flynn was in it.

Ann shifted toward the door, her eyes settling on a point somewhere beyond Flynn's shoulder. "I guess I'll let you two get on with your picnic. I . . . I'm sorry about what my father did."

"Where are you going? I thought the three of us had planned this extravaganza of hot dogs and indigestion."

Her eyes flickered to his face and then away. "I didn't think I'd be welcome."

Flynn caught her arm as she moved closer to the door, pulling her forward until she stood right in front of him. There was nowhere to look but at him. She stared at his collarbone, too ashamed to meet his eyes.

"Ann, you can't possibly think I blame you for what your father did? It had nothing to do with you. I know that."

His voice was so gentle that Ann had to blink back tears. It had been a long time since anyone had used that tone with her. It made her want to lean her head on his chest and let him take care of her.

"How can you be so nice about it? If I hadn't told my father about Becky, he wouldn't have called the social worker and you wouldn't be about to lose Becky."

"Don't be silly." He gave her a gentle shake that brought her eyes to his face. "You couldn't have known what your father was going to do. And I'm *not* going to lose Becky. *We're* not going to lose Becky. Hey, you've got to cultivate a more positive attitude."

Ann managed a shaky smile, but she couldn't prevent the single tear that slipped down her cheek. Flynn's eyes darkened, his expression softening almost magically. His head lowered, and Ann closed her eyes as he kissed the tear from her cheek. It was a gentle gesture, a comforting gesture and yet, somehow, comfort was not exactly what it achieved. With the touch of his mouth on her cheek, the atmosphere was charged with sexual awareness. As if the awareness had been there all along, just waiting for an excuse to break through.

He hesitated, his mouth against her skin, and Ann forgot how to breathe. His lips shifted, trailing along her jaw, drawing closer to her mouth. Ann's mouth softened, anticipating the touch of his. He was so close. So close.

"Are you kissing Ann?"

Flynn jerked as if slapped. Ann's eyes flew open as he stepped away. Was it her imagination or was his breathing a little uneven, his color a little high? His eyes locked on hers for an instant, but it was impossible to read their expression. And then he looked away, and Ann could almost believe that she'd imagined the entire incident.

"Becky. You got your jacket."

"'Course I got my jacket. I thought we was going to the park." The look she gave him made it clear that he was acting slow-witted. Flynn flushed.

"We are. But Ann has to go and get her shoes and I've got to get the picnic."

"You said you was going to do that when you told me to get my jacket."

"Well, yes, I got distracted."

"What's 'stracted mean?"

"HOW DO KIDS MANAGE to ask so many questions?" Flynn's tone was exaggeratedly weary, and Ann hid a smile.

"How else are they going to learn?"

"It just seems like they try to learn everything all at once."

Ann looked to where Becky was playing with a group of other children.

"I think that's the first time I've seen her with kids her age."

Flynn's eyes followed hers, settling on Becky's brightly clad figure. "I think she and her mother moved a lot. According to the investigator, they've had six different addresses in the last two years. I doubt if Becky's had a chance to make any friends."

"Has she ever talked about her father?"

Flynn shook his head, reaching for a bite of cotton candy from the cone Ann held. "She hasn't said much. I get the feeling her mother didn't want to talk about him."

"She told me that Frankie was a present from her father and that book she has was his. That's not a cheap edition of Robert Louis Stevenson and it's part of a set. And Frankie isn't a dime store stuffed toy. He's Steiff."

"Steiff? What's Steiff?"

"They make toys. Expensive toys. Collectible toys. The tag is gone but they always put a button in the animal's ear. If her father bought her Frankie, he probably wasn't on the dole line."

"Maybe he stole him."

"Maybe. I can't help but wonder where he is. I can't imagine what kind of a man would abandon his own child."

"Happens all the time. Here." Ann opened her mouth automatically, her thoughts on other things. She was unaware of the intimacy of Flynn feeding her a bite of sticky cotton candy, or of the way his eyes watched her tongue come out to lick the sugar from her lips.

"You're very good with her."

"With Becky? She's easy to get along with." He shrugged off the compliment, pulling off another length of spun sugar.

"You'd make a good father." His eyes went to Becky again.

"At least I know what not to do. You don't pigeonhole your kids from birth. You don't expect a kid to be perfect. I watched what that did to my brother.

Always striving to be exactly what Dad wanted, never feeling like he'd quite measured up."

"What about you?"

"Me? Well, there are advantages to being the black sheep of the family. No one expects anything but trouble out of you." His smile took on a wicked edge. "I was pretty good at living up to those expectations."

He held another bite of cotton candy up to her mouth, and Ann hesitated a moment before taking it from him. They were slipping into dangerous intimacy. His fingers brushed her lips.

Ann felt the sticky sweet melt on her tongue, her eyes never leaving his. It wasn't fair that he should have such blue, blue eyes. It was too easy to get lost in them. The sounds of the park faded into the background. His fingers shifted but didn't leave her face. His hand cupped her cheek, his thumb brushing across her skin.

"You have the softest skin."

Any second now, she was going to make some light remark and draw away. Any second now. But she couldn't seem to move. "I do?"

"Umm." His eyes dropped to her mouth and Ann felt her pulse pick up. It wasn't fair. He shouldn't be able to do that with just a look. "Did you know you have cotton candy on your mouth?"

"I do?" The words were breathy. She couldn't get enough air. His head was lowering and she should be moving away. She didn't want this. Didn't want it at all. Which explained the quivery sensation in the pit of her stomach when his breath touched her mouth.

Her eyes fell shut. His tongue came out, delicately licking the sticky sweetness from her mouth. The touch was so intimate, so hungry that Ann forgot all about not wanting it. Forgot all the reasons she couldn't get involved with him. Forgot everything but the surprising hunger in her own body. She was the one who moved closer. Her hands came up to rest on the front of his light jacket.

Flynn groaned, a low rumbling sound that Ann felt in every pore of her body. Her mouth opened, inviting him inside, and he took the invitation, sweeping her breath away as his mouth closed over hers, his tongue sliding inside, hot with demand.

They were standing under the huge branches of a live oak, the ancient tree sheltering them, giving the illusion of privacy. Ann wasn't sure how it happened but suddenly she was pressed against the tree, the bark rough against her back, Flynn's body a sensual weight against her.

Her hands slid around his neck, pulling him closer. She felt as if all her life she'd been only half alive and suddenly he'd awakened the sleeping half of her. She'd never known such a rush of urgency, of need. Of hunger.

The passion that flared between them was instantaneous, catching them both off guard, leaving no room for pretense, no room for anything but each other.

"Mr. Flynn, you've got cotton candy in your hair."

Ann felt as if she'd just been pushed out of an airplane without a parachute. The return to reality was so abrupt that she was disoriented. Flynn's head came up, his eyes meeting hers for a moment before he stepped away, leaving her to lean limply against the tree. If it hadn't been for its support, she would have simply slid to the ground. There didn't seem to be any stiffening in her knees.

"How come Ann put cotton candy in your hair?" Becky's piping question was another rude introduction to reality. Ann stared at the little girl for a moment, and then her eyes dropped to the crushed paper cone in her hand. The pale pink confection was almost gone but she'd forgotten all about it when Flynn kissed her. He ran his hand over the back of his head, drawing it back with a grimace.

"I think I need a shower."

Ann nodded, still dazed. He wasn't the only one. She wondered if there was a shower long enough and cold enough to slow her pulse down to normal.

Chapter Seven

"How come the water comes out hot?" Ann looked
from Becky to the stream of water splashing into the
tub and tried to organize her thoughts. It had been like
that all afternoon. No matter how she scolded herself
for letting one little kiss throw her off balance, she
couldn't seem to get back to the real world.

Of course, calling it "one little kiss" was rather like
calling King Kong a spider monkey. A little kiss didn't
send shock waves to your toes. A little kiss didn't leave
you tingling hours later. A little kiss—

"Ann?" She blinked and smiled at Becky.

"They heat the water in a big tank and pump it up
to the faucet." As basic explanations went, it was
about as basic as they came but she wasn't up to trying
to explain the miracles of modern plumbing, even if
she understood them, which she didn't. Becky seemed
satisfied and she climbed into the tub without asking
another question.

Becky was quite capable of taking a bath without a
supervisor, but it had become a nightly ritual for Ann
to sit in the bathroom with her. It was hard to say who
enjoyed the ritual more. Ann tried not to think about
what was going to happen when Becky's mother was

finally found. She couldn't pretend anymore that life was going to go back to the way it had been before she'd opened her door to Flynn's towel-clad, panic-stricken presence.

She reached out to tuck a strand of Becky's hair out of the way of the washcloth. Becky smiled at her, revealing a gap where a tooth had come out two days ago. Ann smiled back, hoping the little girl wouldn't notice the shimmer of tears in her eyes. Flynn had been so nervous when Ann had checked the loose tooth and announced that it was time to pull it.

He'd let her do the honors, telling Becky that since Ann was a doctor, she'd know how to do it just right. When the moment finally came and the tooth was pulled, Ann thought Flynn might cry right along with Becky. But the tears lasted only a moment, more from fright than actual pain. Afterward, they'd made a ritual out of placing the tooth under Becky's pillow for the tooth fairy. Becky had explained that there wasn't really a tooth fairy, but the pragmatic words didn't quite match the excitement in her eyes.

Ann's smile widened as she reached for the washcloth to scrub Becky's back. It had taken her almost ten minutes to convince Flynn that a dollar was enough for a tooth. If she hadn't been there, he would probably have left the Ferrari under Becky's pillow.

"Are you and Mr. Flynn going to get married?" The washcloth slipped and Ann almost fell into the tub.

"What?"

"Are you and Mr. Flynn going to get married?" Becky wound the spring on a toy boat and set it sailing across the tub.

"What on earth would make you ask that?" Ann hoped the amusement in her voice sounded light and not hysterical.

"He was kissing you today."

"Becky, you know people don't get married just because they kiss each other."

"Why do they get married?"

"Well, they get married because they want a home and a family, something to come back to every night. Somebody who'll love them no matter what and be there when they're happy or when they're sad."

"Don't you want those things?"

Ann stared down at Becky, meeting the innocent question in those clear gray eyes. "I don't know. I guess I've never really given it much thought. I've had to work very hard at my job. I guess everybody wants those things but it's not easy to find them."

Becky rubbed soap over the washcloth, lathering it up until the cloth all but disappeared in bubbles. "Mama says that if you really want something, you've got to go out and get it. She says you can't sit around waitin' for stuff to come to you." She scrubbed the soapy cloth over her face.

Ann watched her. Out of the mouths of babes. Surely that statement had to have been designed for Becky.

HALF AN HOUR LATER, Becky was dressed in a long cotton nightgown and tucked into bed. Ann dropped a kiss on her forehead, trying not to think of how much she'd grown to care for this small scrap of humanity.

"Tell me a story, Mr. Flynn." This, too, had become a nightly ritual. Ann moved quietly around the room putting away the day's accumulation of clothes and toys, while Flynn's voice spun a quiet story about elves and princesses and beautiful moths that flew them through fairyland.

The story was only half over when Flynn's voice stopped, and Ann turned to see that Becky had fallen asleep, her lashes making dark crescents against her flushed cheeks. Flynn eased himself off the bed and dropped a kiss on Becky's forehead. They tiptoed from the room, leaving the door open just a crack.

In the living room, the atmosphere was suddenly awkward. The early autumn temperature had dipped low enough that Flynn felt justified in lighting a fire, and it hissed quietly in the fireplace. One lamp burned next to the sofa, casting a pool of brilliance that seemed too intimate.

"Join me in a glass of wine?"

Ann glanced at him and then looked away. He was altogether too sexy. He'd washed the cotton candy out of his hair, and it now fell onto his forehead in a heavy black wave that made her fingers twitch with the urge to push it back. His jeans molded his thighs, just snug enough to tantalize anyone with the least imagination. His shirt was plain blue cotton, but the top two buttons were undone, allowing a glimpse of curling black hair.

It would be foolish to stay for a glass of wine, and one thing Ann had never been was foolish.

"That sounds nice."

Ten minutes later, the two of them were seated on the thick carpeting in front of the fireplace. Huge pillows bolstered their backs. It was a warm, intimate setting and part of Ann couldn't believe that she was here, courting disaster like this. But that was the practical Ann, who'd spent her life working toward certain goals.

There was another Ann, the Ann that was beginning to realize how much she'd given up to ambition. The Ann that wondered about all the things she'd told Becky that went into marriage. That was the Ann sitting here. Besides, where was the danger in sharing a simple glass of wine?

She stared into the fireplace, afraid to look at Flynn, afraid to look too closely at what she was doing. Afraid to stay and even more afraid to go.

Flynn's hand came out and took the wineglass from her fingers. Ann watched him set it on the hearth. The pale liquid picked up all the colors of the fire, bending them into new displays of light and color. Flynn's glass joined hers, the two of them sitting side by side. And still she sat there, her hands lying in her lap, her eyes on the two glasses.

She felt his hands in her hair, pulling out the pins one by one. She should say something. She couldn't just sit here and do nothing. She couldn't just let him... The last pin came out slowly, as if he were dragging out the anticipation. She closed her eyes as her hair tumbled onto her shoulders.

He didn't move, didn't speak until, at last, she could bear the tension no more. She opened her eyes, turning her head until she could see his face. She needed to know what he was thinking.

His eyes were on her hair, deep red waves that made the fire pale in comparison. The flames cast shadows over his features, making it difficult to read his expression.

"You are so beautiful." His voice was husky, soft. "I wanted to see you with your hair down the first moment I saw you. You looked so cool and disapproving but there was such fire in your hair." His fingers slid into the thick waves and Ann shut her eyes again. His thumb brushed her earlobe and she shivered. She felt him shifting closer. Her lips parted, anticipating, needing, wanting.

And then he was there.

His mouth claimed hers hungrily, with none of the tentative searching that had been in his other kisses. They both knew the time for questions was gone. There might be new questions tomorrow, but tonight there was only the two of them.

The spark that had been kindled earlier had lain waiting, needing only a touch to burst into life. Flynn's fingers slid deep into her hair, cupping the back of her head, tilting her mouth to his.

Ann moaned low in her throat as her lips opened, welcoming the invasion of his tongue. He tasted of wine. He tasted of madness. He tasted of all the things she denied herself for so many years. Things she'd only dreamed of. Her tongue came up to meet his, as hungry as he was. They tangled in erotic love play, testing, teasing, savoring.

She was barely aware of his hands shifting to her shoulders, lowering her to the thick carpeting. His mouth left hers but only to taste the delicate skin along her jaw. The firelight created dancing red shadows against her closed eyes. Flynn's mouth slid down her throat, his tongue tasting the pulse that beat frantically at its base.

His fingers teased open the buttons on her blouse, spreading the thin cotton fabric out around her body. When he lifted himself away from her, Ann's eyes fluttered open. She should have felt self-conscious,

Look what we've got for you:

Get 4 FREE full-length Harlequin American Romance® novels.

Plus this handy compact manicure set

Plus a surprise free gift

▼ PLUS LOTS MORE! MAIL THIS CARD TODAY ▼

Harlequin's Best-Ever "Get Acquainted" Offer

Yes, I'll try the Harlequin Reader Service under the terms outlined on the opposite page. Send me 4 free Harlequin American Romance® novels, a free compact manicure set and a free mystery gift.

154 CIH NA9W

PLACE STICKER FOR 6 FREE GIFTS HERE

NAME _____

ADDRESS _____ APT. _____

CITY _____

STATE _____ ZIP CODE _____

PRINTED IN U.S.A.

Don't forget...

...Return this card today to receive your 4 free books, free compact manicure set and free mystery gift.

...You will receive books before they're available in stores and at a discount off retail prices.

...No obligation. Keep only the books you want, cancel anytime.

If offer card is missing, write to: Harlequin Reader Service,
901 Fuhrmann Blvd., P.O. Box 1867, Buffalo, NY 14269-1867

lying beneath him with only the fragile lace of her bra shielding her breasts from his gaze. But the look in his eyes was warm, melting away her inhibitions, her fears, leaving her feeling wanted, loved.

"You are so beautiful." He breathed the words out as if he could hardly believe that she was lying here beneath him.

Her fingers came up to smooth the hair back from his forehead. It promptly slipped back down again, but her hands had moved to other things. His shirt buttons slid apart easily, baring his muscled chest. Ann could feel him watching her but she kept her eyes on her fingers, concentrating on sliding each button loose. If she looked at him, she might lose the fragile courage she'd found.

The shirt at last fell loose and she set her palms against his chest. The crisp curls tickled her palms. He was warm, so warm. She slid her hands up his chest, feeling the shudder that ran through him as her fingertips grazed his flat nipples. She felt powerful. For the first time, she realized the power of her femininity. Flynn actually trembled when she touched him. It was a heady feeling. But she didn't have long to savor the feeling, because Flynn soon showed her that it worked both ways.

His fingers mastered the front clasp of her bra and Ann's nails dug into his chest as she felt it slip loose. Her eyes swept up to meet his and were caught and held in the brilliant blue fires that burned there. He kept his eyes on hers as he opened the lace garment, brushing it aside without really touching her.

His hand rested between her breasts, unmoving, so close without touching. The tension grew as she waited for him to move. Her palms tingled where they touched him, her breathing was shallow. *Why didn't he move?* Just when she thought she would surely explode, he moved.

His eyes never left hers as his hand shifted slowly, so slowly, his fingers hovering over her for an instant before his thumb stroked ever so gently across the tip of her breast. Ann hadn't even realized that she was holding her breath until it left her in a sigh that came perilously close to a sob. Her eyes fell shut, her entire being concentrated on that one tiny point as he captured her nipple between thumb and forefinger and tugged lightly.

"Please." The word was a whisper, almost lost in the crackle of the fire. Her back arched, begging, demanding. And the demand was answered. His head dipped and her fingers buried themselves in his hair as his mouth closed around the swollen point. He seemed to know just what she needed, far more clearly than she herself knew. She felt the tugging at her breast but she felt it more deeply, setting up pulsing waves low in her stomach.

Her hips moved in unconscious invitation, seeking something to fill the aching void that had settled inside. Flynn continued to suckle at her breast, his free hand sliding across the satiny skin of her abdomen. The snap of her jeans popped loose, and then the zipper rasped downward and his fingers were sliding beneath the stiff denim. His hand came to rest over the very heart of her need, only the satin of her panties separating them.

Ann stiffened as his fingers stroked her dewy flesh through the thin fabric. His touch was so intimate, the feeling so intense, it was almost painful. He seemed to understand, because he didn't move to deepen the caress until he felt the tension ease.

When she relaxed beneath him, his fingers moved again, stroking, probing, teasing, all with that frustrating layer of cloth between them. His mouth nuzzled between her breasts and she arched upward against his hand, a moan escaping her. He was so close. So close. She felt him smile against her breasts and a sudden spurt of rage made her dig her nails into his shoulders.

He laughed, the merest ghost of masculine triumph brushing her skin. Before the sound could fan her frustration higher, his hand lifted, sliding beneath the waistband of her panties. Ann's breath came out in a sob as he touched her at last, stroking the delicate folds.

Her body arched as he fanned the flames inside her higher and higher, pushing her toward some goal she was half afraid to reach. But, where he'd made allowances for her uncertainties a moment ago, now he was ruthlessly determined to push her forward. His mouth closed over hers, his tongue stabbing within at the same time that his finger slipped inside her, his thumb pressing on the most sensitive part of her.

Ann felt as if she were suddenly spinning apart. The pleasure caught her, lifted her and then dropped her to fall endlessly through space. She was blind, helpless, with nothing to cling to except Flynn's broad shoulders. He held her tight, his mouth and hands gentle on her trembling body, easing her back down from the heights.

She opened dazed eyes as he stood up, bending to lift her in his arms. The fire continued to burn on the hearth, the flames lower now. Her eyes met Flynn's, reading the hunger that still burned in him, and she buried her face against his bare shoulder, oddly shy in the face of his need.

He carried her easily, kicking the door of his bedroom shut behind them. He set her on the bed and then returned to the door, flicking the lock shut, reminding Ann that they were not alone in the apartment. Her cheeks warmed when she remembered her total abandonment of a few minutes ago. The possibility of being interrupted had been the last thing on her mind.

The room was lit only by one small lamp that burned on a table near the bed. In the dim light, Flynn looked intimidatingly large. She could feel his eyes on her, but she couldn't bring herself to meet them. She stared at his chest as he shrugged out of the loosened shirt and let it fall to the floor. His fingers went to his belt buckle, and Ann felt the color come up in her cheeks at the sight of his arousal blatantly pressed against the heavy denim. She shut her eyes as his jeans hit the floor.

Flynn hesitated, staring at her. She was so still. Was she having second thoughts? He left his shorts on and crossed the room to kneel in front of her.

"Ann?" Her eyelids fluttered but didn't lift, and he cupped her chin, tilting her face to his. "Ann? Look at me, love. You're not afraid of me, are you?"

Her lashes lifted slowly, and he felt as if he could lose himself in the smoky green depths of her eyes. There were so many emotions in her face. Uncertainty, desire and a slumberous look that made his muscles tighten. He bent forward to kiss her and her mouth softened instantly, welcoming him, reassuring him.

Need burned in him. He wanted to bury himself in her, soothing his aching body in the warmth of her. He contented himself with kissing away the tension he could feel, easing her clothes away so slowly she was hardly aware of them going.

When she at last lay naked beneath him, he thought he would surely explode with hunger. He'd had fantasies about how she would look in his bed. The reality far surpassed anything he could have imagined. Her skin was creamy pale, like the finest satin, cool to look at but hot beneath his touch. Her hair spread like fiery silk across his pillow. And her eyes. Her eyes seemed to burn into his very soul.

He could feel her uncertainty as his hands stroked her body, stroking the slumbering fires to new life. If she'd thought it was impossible to want again so soon, he was determined to prove her wrong. He heard the surprised catch in her breathing as his fingers worked magic. She arched beneath him, tangling her fingers in his hair.

The pleading tug of her hands stripped away the last of Flynn's fragile control. He fumbled in the drawer of the nightstand, thinking of her protection though he knew she was long past any clear thoughts. He slid his body over hers, feeling her stiffen and then melt as she felt the heat that burned in him.

Her legs opened, cradling him, welcoming him. He tested himself against her, resting his weight on his hands so that he could watch her face. Her eyes reflected wild uncertainty and her body stiffened for a moment as he slid inside her. He shuddered as she sheathed him. She felt so good, so right. The uncertainty left her eyes, replaced by surprised pleasure and her body softened beneath him. Flynn groaned, lowering himself so that his chest was a sensuous weight on her breasts.

He began to move, slowly, savoring the feel of her tight warmth. Ann matched his movements, clumsily at first, gradually picking up the rhythm, drawing another groan from him. The hunger had been building for so long that the fulfillment could not last long. Flynn felt the delicate contractions grip her body and he moaned a protest. He wanted it to last forever and then his own climax took him, sending him spinning after her into a place where the only reality was each other.

The return to earth was slow. Flynn lifted his head, feeling as if the entire world had been rearranged in the last few minutes. Ann lay still beneath him, her body lax, her face utterly peaceful. He kissed her, tasting her satisfaction in the softness of her mouth. He made to move away and her hands tightened on his hips.

"Don' go." The protest was slurred.

Flynn smiled, kissing her again. "I'll smash you."

He pulled away, seeing the faint moue of discomfort as he withdrew. His brows drew together as a vague suspicion began to form.

"Ann?"

"Umm?" She didn't open her eyes, didn't shift from her sprawled position.

"I have this funny feeling that you've never done this before."

He couldn't have gotten more results if he'd dropped a bomb in the middle of the bedroom. Her eyes flew open, her body tightened, all the lazy pleasure leaving her. She scrambled to pull the sheet over her, tucking it around her breasts defensively. He almost regretted the question. Her reaction gave him his answer even before she spoke.

"What makes you say that?"

He leaned on one elbow next to her, drawing one finger down her bare arm. "It wasn't an accusation, love." He smiled, coaxing her to relax again.

"I'm thirty years old. It isn't likely that I'd still be a...a..."

"Virgin? Ann, it's all right. Why are you so defensive about it?"

Her eyes shifted away from him. "It's ridiculous."

"It's surprising but not ridiculous. Nothing about you could ever be ridiculous."

"You don't think that I'm...frigid or repressed or something?"

"Haven't you heard? There's no such thing as a frigid woman. Only an inept lover." His mouth brushed her shoulder and she shivered. He felt some of the tension ease from her.

"It's not that I have anything against sex, you know. It's just that I never had time for it. I don't mean that exactly. It's just that I've always felt like I had to prove that I'm worthy and I've worked so hard that I've never really had time to get close to other people."

Flynn's mouth cut off the tangled explanation, kissing her until he felt her soften, her hands coming up to clasp his shoulders. He wanted to go out and find her father and beat him to a pulp. Though the name hadn't been mentioned, he knew who it was that Ann was trying to prove her worth to. But he said nothing to her.

When he finally let her up for air, he was pleased with the slightly glazed look in her eyes. She looked like a woman who'd been well and thoroughly loved. The look pleased him.

"You don't owe me any explanations. But you should have told me sooner. I might have taken more time."

The look she gave him was half-shy, half-bawdy and all female. "If you'd taken any more time, I'd have exploded. You made it wonderful for me, Flynn. Thank you."

Flynn felt the color rise in his face. Blushing! She actually had him blushing. He laughed self-consciously. "Don't thank me. Believe me, the pleasure was all mine."

He slid his arm beneath her shoulders, pulling her to his side. Ann's head snuggled into his shoulder, feeling so right that he wondered how he'd ever slept without her small body tucked against his. She was asleep within minutes.

It wasn't quite that easy for Flynn. Lying there, staring into the dimly lit room, he wondered at the changes that had overtaken his life. Three weeks ago, he'd had nothing more important on his mind than whether or not to fly to Switzerland for the ski season. Now, here he was with a little girl who looked to him to take care of her and Ann.

Just what was he going to do about Ann? He didn't even know what he *wanted* to do about Ann. Somehow, she'd gone from being his beautiful but hostile neighbor to feeling so right in his bed that he couldn't imagine doing without her.

He turned his head, inhaling the faint herbal scent of her hair. Making love to her had been like nothing he'd ever experienced before. She'd felt so good. He'd never found such total satisfaction in a woman. He reached up to shut out the light. Nothing could be decided tonight.

Tonight, he just wanted to savor the closeness, the warmth of her in his bed.

Chapter Eight

Ann woke up suddenly, with the feeling of panic that comes of knowing that you're not in your own bed but not knowing where you are. Realization came quickly but it did little to slow the pounding of her heart. She shifted gingerly, easing away from Flynn's hold until she could sit up.

Flynn continued to sleep as she gathered up her clothes and dressed. Her movements were furtive, as if she were a thief in the night. She snapped her jeans and jerked her shirt on, thrusting buttons through buttonholes without paying much attention to whether she was matching the right button with the right buttonhole.

She stole quick glances at Flynn, terrified that he would wake up before she could slip away. She couldn't face him right now. It was foolish, childish even, but she just needed to get away.

Once dressed, she hesitated for a moment, unable to resist the chance to study him when she didn't have to worry about those brilliant blue eyes watching her. In sleep, he looked younger than his thirty-three years. His mouth was softer, more vulnerable. His hair fell onto his forehead in that tantalizing black lock, and she clenched her fingers against the urge to push it back off his forehead.

The sheet lay draped across his waist, exposing the mat of curling dark hair that covered his chest. She flushed, remembering the feel of those crisp curls against her body. Her breasts tingled at the memory. Her eyes followed the line of hair as it tapered across his stomach and disappeared beneath the sheet. She flushed again as the line of her thoughts moved beyond what the sheet revealed.

Part of her wanted to climb back into bed and wake him. She wanted to find out if it was possible to know the kind of pleasure she remembered from the night just past. Surely, she must have dreamed the total satisfaction she'd felt. She backed away, physically resisting temptation. She hurried from the room, carefully shutting the door behind her.

It was early. The light outside the balcony doors had the watery quality of dawn. The fire had burned to ashes on the hearth, not even a glowing ember to show what had been the night before. Ann picked up her shoes, trying not to think of what had begun here and ended in the bedroom.

Letting herself into her own apartment, she had a feeling of unreality. Oscar trotted toward her, meowing low in his throat, a questioning greeting. Ann wondered if he could see that something was different about her and then scolded herself for the foolish thought. The only thing Oscar could see was that she was home and it was morning and he was ready to be fed.

Ten minutes later, she stood in front of the mirror in her bedroom. Oscar was happily devouring his cat food and the apartment was still. The Ann who looked at her from out of the glass wasn't the Ann she'd known for thirty years. There was a new knowledge in her eyes. An awareness that hadn't been there before.

She looked away from her reflection, uncomfortable with what she saw there, unwilling to deal with the changes just yet. She'd get dressed and go to the hospital. It was early but there was always work to be done. And, right now, she wanted to lose herself in work.

FLYNN CAME AWAKE SLOWLY, feeling at peace with himself and the world in general. His hand went out but found only empty space. He opened his eyes, knowing that Ann was gone. A hint of her shampoo clung to the pillows, bringing vivid memories of how soft she'd felt in his arms.

He was disappointed that she was gone but a little relieved, too. This would give him a chance to figure out what he was going to say to her when they met again. Were they now lovers in the full sense of the word, or was she going to see last night as something that happened once but never again?

He wanted to be her lover. It surprised him to realize how badly he wanted that. He wanted her back in his bed, in his arms. He wanted to wake up next to her in the morning.

He got up and walked into the bathroom, turning the shower on full force and stepping under the warm spray. Becky would be up soon, if she wasn't up already. One thing he'd learned over the past weeks was that children didn't understand the idea of sleeping late. Mornings were for getting up, no matter what had gone the night before.

Becky. She'd been the catalyst to bring him and Ann together, but it was no longer possible to pretend that she was all that connected them.

Half an hour later, he left his bedroom and walked, barefoot, into the living room. Ann's shoes were gone but the pillows still lay on the floor in front of the fireplace and their wineglasses still stood on the wide hearth. He picked up the glasses and then turned at a sound behind him.

Becky stood in the hall doorway, her eyes stern with disapproval. "It's awful early to be drinking, Mr. Flynn. Are you going to get plastered again?"

Flynn grinned at her, not in the least put out by her scolding tone. "I haven't had a drop, urchin. These are from last night. Hungry?"

"Starved."

"Well, go comb your hair and I'll see what I can do about finding you some breakfast."

WHEN THE KNOCK ON THE DOOR CAME, Ann jumped, spilling milk on the counter. She grabbed a sponge to mop up the puddle, grimacing at the fine tremor in her hand. She'd known that she wouldn't be able to avoid Flynn forever. In fact, she'd known that she wouldn't even be able to avoid him all evening. But she hadn't expected him to come knocking on her door when she'd been home less than twenty minutes.

He was going to want to talk about last night and she wasn't ready to talk about it. She wasn't sure she'd ever be ready. This was one problem she hadn't been able to put aside by going to work. It had nagged at the back of her mind all day, like an aching tooth that couldn't be ignored.

The knock came again, and she dropped the sponge into the sink.

"I'll just tell him that I don't want to talk about it. After all, what's to discuss? We made love. People do it all the time. No big deal."

Oscar gave her a dubious look, as if he didn't believe her words any more than she did.

She pulled open the door to find Flynn's hand raised to knock a third time. All her carefully selected phrases flew out of her head when she saw his face.

He looked old and tired. Deep lines bracketed his mouth, and there was a dull hurt in his eyes. He was far removed from the man she'd left sleeping only twelve hours ago.

"My God, Flynn. What's wrong?"

"They found Becky's mother. She's dead."

"YOU'RE SURE BECKY IS all right alone?" Ann handed Flynn a cup of coffee.

"Thanks. Becky is plugged into a tape of *Return of the Jedi*. I don't think she'll come up for air for another hour, at least. I left the door open and she knows where we are if she needs something."

He took a swallow of the coffee, staring into the cup broodingly. "I just don't know how to tell her."

"I know." Ann sat down across from him with her own cup. "Tell me what Ms. Davis had to say."

"She came by this afternoon. I sent Becky out onto the balcony so we could talk. She said that they'd found Becky's mother. At first, I didn't know whether to be glad or sorry. I mean, I was glad for Becky's sake but I figured it meant that I was going to lose her and she sort of grows on you."

"I know." She did know. The thought of Becky going out of her life was a painful one.

Flynn set the cup down and leaned his head back against the chair, his face so weary that Ann wanted to smooth the lines away.

"Anyway, before I could say much of anything, she told me that Becky's mother had been found dead."

"Oh God. Poor little Becky. What happened to her? Do they know?"

He shook his head. "It's too soon to know much yet. All I know is that they found her body in one of the aqueducts. I guess they'll have to do an autopsy."

"Are they sure it's her?"

"The identification in the purse is hers and the landlady went in and gave positive ID just a couple of hours ago."

"Poor Becky."

There didn't seem to be anything else to say. After a long silence, Ann stirred, trying to gather her thoughts into some practical pattern.

"What did Ms. Davis say about Becky staying with you? They're not going to take her away now, are they?"

"No. She said that, under the circumstances, she thinks it would be cruel to remove Becky from our care. Becky feels safe here."

"That's something at least."

He stirred restlessly. "Not much in the face of her mother's death. And it's only temporary. They're going to try and find some record of Becky's father and contact him. If they can't find him or he doesn't want her, then she'll be put in a foster home."

Flynn surged to his feet, his long strides eating up the distance between sofa and door and then back again. Ann watched him, uncertain of what to say to reassure him.

"You know, it isn't like the days of Jane Eyre. A lot of foster parents are really wonderful people."

"Sure. But what if she gets foster parents who aren't wonderful people? You know, she acts real tough on the outside but she's still just a little girl."

"I know." She watched him pace back and forth, his strides quick with pent up frustrations. "Maybe you could be her foster parent."

Flynn stopped and spun to face her so suddenly that Ann jumped. His eyes pinned her to the chair, bright blue with emotion. "Do you think I haven't thought of that? But what do I know about kids? I'm a bachelor. I don't even have a respectable job. Besides, a little girl needs a mother. And it wouldn't matter anyway because Davis made it clear that she had to work very hard convincing her superiors to let Becky stay with me. The only reason that they aren't taking her away immediately is because my parents have spotless reputations and she told them that Becky and I would be spending most of our time with them.

"Even that wouldn't have done it if she hadn't implied that the rest of the time you'd be around to protect Becky's impressionable young mind from any bad influences that I might exert. You'll be pleased to know, Dr. Perry, that your reputation is impeccable. Good thing they don't know that you spent last night in my bed."

The apartment was absolutely silent as they stared at each other. Color flooded Ann's face and then drained away, leaving her ashen. She stared at him for a long moment, hurt in her eyes before she looked away, gathering her defenses around her like a cloak.

"I think—"

"Oh, God, I'm sorry, Ann." He covered the short distance between them in one long stride, dropping to one knee and taking her hands before she had a chance to draw away. "I'm sorry. I shouldn't have said that. I don't even know *why* I said it."

Ann looked anywhere but at his face. She felt very vulnerable and she didn't want him to see that vulnerability. "It's okay." She tugged on her hands but his fingers tightened over hers, denying release.

"No, it's not okay. I didn't mean to sneer about last night. That's the last thing in the world I meant to do. It was special." Unwillingly, her eyes were drawn to his face, reading the absolute sincerity there. Some of the ice that had settled around her heart melted.

"Was it special?" Ann hadn't meant to ask that. It sounded too young, too vulnerable.

His face softened magically, leaving Ann breathless. "It was incredibly special and I had no business throwing it in your face like that."

"It's okay."

"No, it isn't okay. It's just that it was pretty frustrating to realize that the only reason Becky was being allowed to stay with me was because you were around to make me look respectable. I've never thought of myself as quite that much of a rake and roué. I mean, I'm not a dedicated banker or lawyer but I'm hardly Don Juan, either. By the time Ms. Davis was through explaining all the half-truths she had to tell to get them to leave Becky here, I felt more like Jack the Ripper."

Ann's fingers tightened over his before pulling away. This time, he let her go. "It's all right. I know how worried you are about Becky."

"How do you tell a little girl that her mother is dead? That she'll never see her again?" The agony in his face made Ann's heart twist. Without thinking about it, she reached out to smooth the unruly lock of hair back from his forehead.

"We'll do it together. Becky's strong. She'll be okay."

"I just wish there was some way I could protect her from this."

"I know you do, Flynn. I know you do."

JOHN WILLIAMS'S MUSIC BLARED out the finale as Princess Leah, Han Solo, Luke Skywalker and their assorted furry and metallic companions accepted the accolades of the rebel forces. Flynn stared at the screen over Becky's shoulder, wishing that George Lucas could arrange for real life to work out as neatly as it did in the movies. He picked up the remote control and shut the television off as the credits began to roll.

"I love *Star Wars*. When I grow up, I want to be like Han Solo and fly through space. Wouldn't you like to do that, Mr. Flynn?"

She turned to look at him, her face still lit up with the magic of the film, and Flynn had to swallow hard. He dreaded being the one to snuff that light.

"Becky, I need to talk to you."

She stared at him and then her eyes dropped away. Her face closed up, reminding him of the way she'd looked when he'd first found her.

"It's about that lady from the welfare."

"Sort of."

"Are you gonna send me away?"

"No. Of course I'm not going to send you away." He reached out to pick her up, setting her on his lap, feeling the rigidity of her small body, as if she were afraid that if she relaxed, someone would hurt her. "Didn't I promise that I wouldn't send you away?"

"People don't always keep their promises." It was said in such an adult, resigned way that Flynn could only stare at her downcast face. He looked at Ann, seeing the tears swimming in her eyes.

"Becky, I'm not going to send you away but I've got some bad news about your mother." She said nothing, only continued to stare at her hands and Flynn went on, feeling as if he were stumbling hopelessly but not knowing what else to do. "Your mother is dead, honey."

The words sounded so bald, but he didn't know how else to say it. In the quiet that followed his words, the video tape hit the end of its travel and began to rewind, the quiet hiss sounding unnaturally loud.

"You mean dead, like when Charly the cat died?"

"I . . . yes, like when Charly the cat died."

She lifted her head, looking at him out of clear gray eyes. "She won't be coming to get me?"

"She won't be coming to get you."

He waited for the tears. She dropped her head again, her small fingers picking at a spot of lint on her corduroy pants.

"Can I stay here?"

"You can stay here for as long as you'd like." Later, there'd be a time to try and explain about foster homes and adoption. Now, what she needed was some security.

"Can I watch *Jedi* again?"

Flynn stared at her and then looked at Ann. She shrugged, clearly at a loss. "Sure you can, sweetheart. Do you want us to watch it with you?"

"If you want." She slid off his lap and picked up the remote control, pushing the button to turn on the screen and then starting the tape over again.

"Ann and I will be in the kitchen, if you need us."

"Okay."

Once in the other room and safely out of earshot, Flynn turned to look at Ann. "What's wrong with her? Do you think we should call a doctor or something?"

"I *am* a doctor."

"Of course." He thrust his fingers through his hair, ruffling it into wild disarray. "Why didn't she cry or something?"

"She's just a child, Flynn. Death is still a bit abstract to her. It may take a little while for her to realize that her mother is really never coming back."

"I suppose." He raked through his hair again. "I keep thinking there's something I could do to make this easier for her, something I should say."

"You've done the best you can. Now all you can do is be there for her when she needs you."

FLYNN HAD NO IDEA what time it was when he came out of a light sleep, aware that something was wrong. He hadn't been asleep long. He was surprised that he'd fallen asleep at all. After tucking Becky in and telling her the obligatory story, he and Ann had shared a glass of wine and then she'd gone back to her apartment, leaving instructions to call her if he needed her.

Looking in on Becky, he'd experienced a feeling of total unreality. She slept so peacefully, as if this night were no different than any other. Was death really such an abstract concept to a child that she didn't realize what it was going to mean in her life?

But then who was he to question her reaction? Death had been an abstract to him until that night three years ago, when the police had called to tell him that Mark was dead and ask him to identify the body. Staring at his brother's face, forever wiped of emotion, death had ceased to be abstract and had become very real. If it had taken him three decades to understand the reality of death, why should he expect Becky to understand it in less than one?

The sound that had awakened him came again and he slid out of bed, slipping on a black silk robe as he left his bedroom and padded down the dim hallway. Pushing open Becky's door, the sound was clearer, easily identifiable. She was crying.

He crossed the room, easing himself onto the edge of her bed and gathering her shaking body into his arms. Her arms came up to circle his neck and she buried her face in the thin silk over his shoulder.

"It's all right, honey. It's all right."

"Mama. I want Mama." The words were muffled by sobs but Flynn felt them like tiny knives in his heart. "Mama."

"I know you do, sweetheart. I know you do. Cry it all out, honey. I've got you safe."

He had no idea how long she cried. He held her, rocking her, brushing the tangled hair back from her face, murmuring soothingly and wishing that there was something he could do to take her hurt away.

She cried herself to sleep and, even in sleep, her breath came in shaken little sobs. Flynn lifted his long legs onto the bed, easing her into a more comfortable position across his lap and settled his back against the headboard.

He studied her face in the light from the hallway. Her lower lip still quivered with each breath. Her lashes made spiky little patterns against her pale cheeks. She looked like exactly what she was—a frightened little girl whose world had been turned upside down.

Looking at her, he was struck by how right it felt to have her small body cuddled so trustingly against him. His arms tightened and he brushed a kiss against her hot forehead.

He'd never given a whole lot of thought to the matter of fatherhood. If he'd thought about it at all, he figured that being a husband would come first and children would be a much later consideration. But then he'd gotten drunk and stumbled into an alley and come up with a whole new perspective on life.

He didn't want to give up Becky. He didn't want to lose her small presence in his life. He wanted to keep her with him and watch her grow up. And, it wasn't just Becky that he wanted in his life. He wanted a woman to share it with.

He leaned his head back against the headboard and closed his eyes, feeling exhaustion creep over him. It had been one hell of a day.

"MR. FLYNN, what does being dead mean?"

Flynn dropped the spoon into the pancake batter and then reached in to fish it out, stalling for time. Becky had been unusually quiet this morning but, other than that, nothing seemed to have changed. Of the two of them, he wondered if he wasn't having a harder time coping with her mother's death than she was. And then a question like that came out of the blue.

He set the spoon in the sink and turned the heat off under the griddle. Wiping his hands on a towel as he moved over to the table, he sat down opposite the little girl. How was he supposed to answer a question like that?

"Well, when someone dies, they go out of our lives forever and we don't see them anymore."

Her eyes met his solemnly and he wondered if he'd explained it clearly enough. Should he tell her that her mother was in heaven or would that confuse her more than ever?

"You mean like when Yoda dies in *Return of the Jedi*?"

"Well, yeah, I guess so."

"Will Mama come back and visit me like Yoda visited Luke?"

"I...well..." He thrust his fingers through his hair, wondering how to explain that Yoda was make-believe and that make-believe and real life didn't always work out the same. He moved around the table to the chair next to hers, lifting her onto his lap.

"You won't see your mom like Luke can see Yoda. At least you won't see her standing in front of you and talking to you. But when you think about her and remember her, you'll see her in your mind and that will be sort of like having her there again."

Becky leaned her head against his shoulder, her fingers twisting a button on his shirt. "But, she won't really be there, will she?"

Flynn swallowed hard, his eyes stinging. "No, honey, she won't really be there. But that doesn't mean that she doesn't still love you." He brushed the hair back from her forehead, wishing it were easier to read her thoughts. "You know, it's okay to cry. You can even get mad because we all get mad when someone we love leaves us behind even when we know it wasn't their fault.''

He didn't know if he'd said the right things. He felt woefully inadequate for explaining death and how to deal with it. He'd offered her the simplest of comforts. Surely there was something more to say.

He waited a long time to see if Becky would say anything else, ask any more questions, but she seemed content with his clumsy explanation. When she slid off his lap, he didn't try to hold onto her. Perhaps everyone had to deal with death in their own way, no matter what their age.

Flynn went back to the counter and turned on the griddle again. The last thing in the world he felt like doing was eating breakfast and he wasn't sure if Becky had any interest in food, but it seemed like a reasonable thing to do. He stirred the batter and decided it was too thick. A little milk would help. Turning toward the refrigerator, he bumped into Becky who'd been standing right behind him.

"Sorry, urchin. Would you get the milk for me?"

She went and got the milk carton and handed it to him. He watched her out of the corner of his eye as he splashed milk into the batter and stirred it. Instead of going back to the table, she stood right next to him, watching every move he made.

Without comment, he hooked his foot around a stool and pulled it over to the counter, lifting her up onto it so that she could watch what he was doing.

"Hungry?"

She nodded, watching him flick water onto the griddle to test it. The droplets danced on the cast iron and disappeared instantly. Flynn reached for the bowl and ladle.

"Mama used to make me teddy bear pancakes for breakfast."

It was the first words she'd spoken in several minutes. Flynn hesitated with the ladle in midair. It hadn't been a request but still....

"Teddy bear pancakes?"

She nodded solemnly. "They taste better than regular pancakes."

"Teddy bear pancakes." His tone was flat and resigned. He studied the batter and the griddle, seeking some inspiration. Why hadn't his mother ever made teddy bear pancakes? She should have known that it would be an important skill in his life.

It took numerous failures and most of the batter but, with Becky's coaching and Flynn's imagination, they eventually turned out a credible facsimile of a teddy bear in pancake form. Flynn eyed his masterpiece with great pride as he settled it on the plate in front of his small judge and watched her devour a half hour's work in a few bites.

It was worth the burned knuckles and wasted batter to hear Becky giggle over his clumsy efforts. He dried his hands, watching as she consumed the teddy bear pancake, carefully cutting off first one ear and then the other and working her way down to the legs. Clearly, there was an established pattern to eating a teddy bear.

He stroked his hand over her head and she glanced up, smiling through a mouthful of dough. There was a shadow in the back of her eyes but for now, her world was safe, as long as Flynn was within reach.

Flynn only hoped he could keep it that way.

Chapter Nine

"Dr. Perry to emergency please. Dr. Perry to emergency." The tinny voice echoed over the PA. Ann scribbled her signature on the bottom of a chart and handed it back to the nurse before hurrying down the hall to the elevator.

This had possibly been the worst week of her life. Just when her personal life was demanding more emotional energy than she had to give, her professional life was seeing a surge of unwanted business.

The elevator was empty for once, and she allowed herself the luxury of leaning against one wall and closing her eyes. If she was honest, it wasn't so much that she was any busier than usual. It was just that her heart wasn't really in it these days. A part of her wondered if it ever had been.

She pushed the thought away but it refused to be ignored. It wasn't that her work wasn't important, and it could be very rewarding. It was just that...just what?

Just that she had the feeling that she was living her father's dreams and ambitions instead of her own. He'd been the one to direct her toward medical school and she'd done just what he wanted, pushing aside her own desires to please him. Now she was beginning to wonder just how much she'd given up in an effort to make him love her.

She straightened as the elevator came to a halt and the doors slid open. Now was not the time to try and analyze her entire life—past, present and future. She'd think about it later.

The next chance she had to sit down and think of anything wasn't until late that afternoon. Seated in the staff lounge, a cup of lukewarm coffee in her hand, Ann leaned her head back on the worn sofa and shut her eyes, closing out the buzz of conversation coming from two doctors across the room.

She was so tired. Not physically tired but mentally tired. Tired of thinking, tired of trying to decide what was right, tired of worrying about what her father wanted. She wanted to get up and walk out of the hospital and never come back. She wanted to go home to Flynn and Becky and shut the door and not come out for a month.

Home to Flynn and Becky? Was that how she was beginning to think of it? Dangerous thinking. What were they doing right now? Had they gone to the park, or maybe Becky was watching a movie on the VCR and Flynn was doing more of his endless research on the subject of schooling. The new school year had started two weeks ago, but Ms. Davis had agreed that it might be best for Becky to stay home. It was a difficult time for her. Unspoken was the thought that, when they placed her in a foster home, she probably wouldn't be in the same school district that she was now, anyway. Flynn refused to talk about foster homes.

Flynn. Another subject she'd been avoiding examining. She wasn't sure just what her feelings were, and she was afraid that if she looked too closely she might not like what she found.

They'd made love. It wasn't something that she could ignore or forget. Once in a while, she would look up and catch Flynn watching her and she knew that he hadn't forgotten, either. Just the memory of that night was enough to make her knees feel quivery. What would have happened between them if Becky's needs hadn't taken precedence?

The alarm on her watch pinged discreetly and she sat up, downing the last of her coffee and forcing her mind back to her job. Soon, she was going to have to have a long talk with herself. There were a lot of things she needed to think about. Like the direction her life was going; did she want to spend the rest of her life in medicine; and what would it be like to fall in love with Flynn McCallister?

The next afternoon, she was no closer to answering any of her own questions, but the questions themselves had been pushed aside by more pressing matters. Sitting on Flynn's sofa, she watched him pace back and forth across the living room, his strides full of coiled energy.

"What time is it?"

"It's five minutes later than it was the last time you asked. Flynn, she isn't even due for another five minutes."

"I know. But she might get here early."

"So you're wearing a path in the carpet for her?"

He stopped abruptly, staring down at his feet as if he'd only just realized what he was doing. The smile he gave Ann was rueful. He came and sat down in a chair beside the sofa.

"I'm a little uptight."

"No kidding."

"It's just that Ms. Davis didn't give me any idea of why she wanted to see us."

"Maybe she just wants to check and make sure Becky is all right."

He shook his head. "She was here three days ago."

"Did she say anything then that might give you a clue?"

"Just that they were still looking for Becky's father." He frowned. "I don't know why they're going to all this effort to find him. What kind of a jerk abandons his kid?"

Ann shrugged. "Maybe there's extenuating circumstances."

"Ha!" Before he could expand on his opinion of extenuating circumstances, there was a knock on the door. Their eyes met, each wanting some reassurance that neither of them could give. Flynn grinned and lifted his thumb in a cocky gesture of reassurance, but he didn't feel in the least bit secure.

As he walked to the door, he felt as nervous as if he were walking down the gray corridors leading toward death row. He'd told Joe to send Ms. Davis up when she arrived. Now, he wished he hadn't. If Joe had called first, it would have given him a minute to prepare for whatever she might have to say. None of his feelings showed in his face as he opened the door.

"Come in, Ms. Davis. It looks like you beat the rain here."

She smiled as he took her light jacket and hung it in the coat closet. "Early in the season for rain but it does look like we may get a storm before nightfall."

Flynn followed her into the living room, wishing that he could read something from her face.

"Dr. Perry, I'm glad you could be here. I hope it hasn't put too much of a crimp in your schedule at the hospital."

"Not at all." Ann smiled at the older woman and she wondered if Flynn felt as nervous as she did.

"Would you like some coffee?" He had to force himself to make the polite offer when what he really wanted to do was demand why she was here.

"No, thank you. I'm sure you're both anxious to know the reason for this visit." She sat down, arranging her skirt over her knees.

Flynn forced himself to sit down when every muscle in his body demanded action. "Actually, we were wondering. Was there a problem with your visit Monday?"

"No problem at all, Mr. McCallister. Personally, I've seldom seen any two people more suited to taking care of a child. You've done wonders with Becky."

Flynn smiled, feeling as if his face might crack with the effort that went into the gesture. "Becky is a terrific kid."

"All kids are wonderful. Where is Becky?"

"My mother has her for the afternoon."

"Good." Ms. Davis smoothed her skirts. "I'm afraid I have some good and some bad news."

Flynn smiled slightly. "I've always had a healthy distrust of conversations that start out on that note."

"I'm afraid it won't be possible for you to adopt Becky, Mr. McCallister."

Flynn kept the faint smile pinned in place, aware of Ann's head jerking toward him. He should have told her what he had in mind. But there was no time to explain it to her now. "I didn't expect a decision so quickly. I can't believe that my reputation is so bad that it would earn me an immediate rejection as parental material."

"It really has nothing to do with your reputation, Mr. McCallister."

He leaned forward, his eyes pinning her to her chair with their intensity. "What if I were to get married? Would that help at all?"

His eyes shifted to Ann. She stared at him, feeling her own eyes widen with shock as she realized what he was thinking. If they were married, it might make it possible for them to adopt Becky. She sat back against the cushions, unable to drag her eyes away, unable to believe what she was thinking.

He was suggesting that they marry for Becky's sake. It was a ridiculous idea. Gothic. After all, people didn't marry just for the sake of a child that didn't belong to either one of them.

It was amazing that he could even consider such a thing. It was amazing that she wasn't leaping up and denying any such implication. But what was most surprising was that it hurt to think that he'd be willing to marry her for Becky's sake.

She wanted him to want her for herself.

The thought was so stunning that Ann jerked her eyes away from his, afraid that he might read it in her expression. She stared down at her linked hands, unwilling to even consider the implications of the thought.

"Your bachelorhood really doesn't make any difference, Mr. McCallister. Adoption simply isn't possible. Becky's father has been located and he wants his child."

The words fell into a pool of silence, as if each were a small stone, sending out ripples as they hit the water.

"Her father?" Flynn's voice was dazed. He'd never seriously thought that they'd find the man. "Her father wants her now? Where was he for the last three years? You can't just be a parent when the mood strikes you and then drop it! What's going to happen the next time he decides he doesn't want to be a father? Is Becky going to be sleeping in alleys again? I thought you people were supposed to be concerned that Becky get a good home. And now you're just going to hand her over to some flake who couldn't be bothered with her for the last three years." By the time he finished speaking, he was on his feet, glaring down at the social worker.

Ann wondered how Ms. Davis could look so calm. Flynn was a more than slightly intimidating figure. The clouds had thickened, leaving the apartment lit with a thin gray light. In his anger, Flynn looked enormous, as if the force of his emotions had given him added size. Electricity seemed to crackle around him. Ann was thankful that his rage wasn't directed at her. Ms. Davis was apparently made of sterner stuff.

"I understand your concern, Mr. McCallister. And your disappointment. I know that you wanted to adopt Becky yourself and I can tell you that I would have given you my recommendation if Mr. Traherne hadn't turned up."

"Who's Mr. Traherne?"

"Becky's father."

"Traherne? Becky's last name is Sinclair. If this Traherne couldn't even be bothered to marry Becky's mother, how can he lay any legal claim on Becky?"

"They were married, Mr. McCallister. You see, three years ago Becky's mother left Mr. Traherne and took their child with her. Mr. Traherne has been looking for both of them since but, until our department started a search for Becky's father, he had been unable to locate his wife or his daughter. He did not abandon them."

Flynn sat down slowly, searching for some flaw in her words. "Why did she take Becky and run? She must have had a reason."

"According to Mr. Traherne, they had a misunderstanding. His wife disappeared before they could clear the misunderstanding up."

"She must have been afraid of him to run like that."

"Mr. Traherne's reputation is impeccable. He's a doctor, the Traherne family has been in Denver for over seventy-five years and they are all respected members of the community. We feel that it's in the best interests of the child if she can be with her natural father."

Ms. Davis glanced at her watch and reached for her briefcase. "I have another appointment in half an hour. I assume it's all right with you if Becky stays here until her father arrives. He should be here day after tomorrow."

Flynn roused himself at her words. His smile was strained but he stood up to show her to the door. "I want to thank you for the work you've done on Becky's behalf, Ms. Davis."

"It's my job, Mr. McCallister." Her fingers were warm and dry as they shook hands. "You've done wonders for that little girl. She's very lucky to have met you."

"Oh, I don't know. I feel like I'm the lucky one."

"You'll make a wonderful father when you have children of your own."

He smiled and shut the door behind her. Behind him, he could hear Ann neatening the stacks of children's books that were scattered over the coffee table. He stood in the dim hallway and looked at the wreckage of all his plans.

He was losing Becky. No more horrible coffee, no more trips to the park, no more bedtime stories. The thought brought a hollow ache to his gut. She'd wound her small fingers into his heart and it was going to hurt like hell to pull them loose.

With Becky gone, what was going to happen to his relationship with Ann? Becky was the catalyst that had brought them together. Most of their time had been spent with Becky in tow. They'd had so little time together. He didn't have to close his eyes to remember the one night they'd spent together. The feel of her in his arms, the scent of her on his pillow, those were things that were with him every minute.

When Becky left, would Ann still want to be with him or was he going to lose her, too?

THE NEXT TWO DAYS were strained. Flynn and Ann had decided not to tell Becky about her father. If there was some mistake, there was no sense in getting her hopes up only to have them dashed. There'd been enough disappointments in her young life.

Every time Flynn looked at Becky, he was reminded of how little time was left. Every time he looked at Ann, he saw so many questions that he was afraid to ask.

There was so much left unsettled between them, things that had nothing to do with Becky. Where was their relationship going to go once Becky was gone? They'd made love and then circumstances had parted them as firmly as if they'd been on different continents. Since the death of Becky's mother, there'd been no opportunities to think about the two of them.

Ann had never mentioned his oblique suggestion that they marry in order to adopt Becky. Flynn wondered if she had been mortally offended or if she'd understood and shared his desperation. He wanted to ask her about it, but there never seemed a moment when they could really talk. Or, perhaps, they were both afraid to find out what would happen when they finally didn't have Becky to serve as both link and barrier between them.

But she wouldn't be there much longer. What then?

THE DAY BECKY'S FATHER was supposed to arrive, Ann stayed home from the hospital. The sudden showers that had drenched southern California had given way to more typical sunshine. It was the kind of weather that made visitors to L.A. wonder why anyone would ever live anywhere else. Flynn was not impressed.

All he could think about was the meeting with Traherne. Father or not, he wasn't turning Becky over to the man until he was sure she'd be cared for. Ann occupied herself in the kitchen, baking endless batches of cookies and burning every other panful. Becky had opted to play on the balcony, losing herself among the greenery.

When Joe buzzed up from the lobby to say that there was a Mr. Traherne here, Flynn felt as if the world had come to a halt. He hadn't realized how much he'd been hoping the other man wouldn't show up until this moment.

"Send him on up, Joe."

He turned from the intercom and met Ann's eyes, reading the same uncertainties that he was feeling. He forced himself to smile, wanting to ease some of the tension from her face.

"Hey, how bad can he be?"

The knock on the door came before she could say anything. Flynn gave Ann a thumbs-up and went to answer the door. Ann couldn't make herself follow him. What if Becky's father turned out to be a blustering, obnoxious creep? How could they let Becky go with someone like that? How could they let Becky go at all?

There was a murmur of male voices as Flynn answered the door. Ann had only a second to offer a garbled prayer, not even sure what she was asking for.

"Ann, this is Rafferty Traherne, Becky's father."

Ann offered her hand to the man next to Flynn, trying to keep her surprise from showing in her face. She wasn't sure what she'd expected. Someone not quite so large and... She reached for the right word to describe him and finally came up with solid. Rafferty Traherne was definitely solid.

The first surprise was his hair. For some reason, she'd expected him to share Becky's pale gold coloring. But his hair was gray. Not sprinkled with gray but solid steel. The color was unexpected, the more so when it was easy to see that he was still in his early thirties.

At six foot tall, he had none of Flynn's lean whip-cord strength. He was built like a bulldozer. Broad shoulders and hands that swallowed her own fingers. There was nothing here that reminded her of Becky's delicate bone structure. Nothing to show that he was related at all until she looked into his eyes. They were the same clear gray as his daughter's. And they gave her that same feeling that they could look right into her soul. Something told her that this man would not be easy to lie to.

"How do you do, Mr. Traherne."

"Please, call me Rafferty. I understand you've been taking care of Becky." His voice matched his body. Deep, dark and strong.

"Well, between the two of us, Flynn and I have been looking out for her."

"I appreciate it." His eyes flicked away from her, and Ann knew immediately what he was seeking.

"Becky is outside. We thought it would be best if we had a chance to talk to you before the two of you met."

"Of course." If he was impatient to see his daughter it was impossible to read it in his face, but Ann suspected that Rafferty would never be easy to read.

"Why don't we have a cup of coffee. I know you must have a lot of questions." She looked at Flynn and he nodded.

"Good idea. Have a seat, Traherne. I'll get the coffee."

He disappeared into the kitchen, leaving Ann alone with their guest. She led the way to the fireplace grouping, seating herself on the sofa and watching him sink into one of the chairs. Like Flynn, he dominated the overstuffed piece of furniture without effort.

"How is Becky? All they told me was that she was in good health."

"Becky is wonderful. She's bright and very mature for her age."

Flynn came in, setting a tray of cups on the coffee table. "Becky is a great little girl. She deserves a solid home."

Ann flushed at the edge of hostility in his voice, but Rafferty seemed to take it in stride. "I never intended for her to have anything else. I can understand your concern. From what Ms. Davis told me, you've done an awful lot for Becky."

Flynn picked up a coffee cup and settled into the other chair, stretching his long legs out in front of him. He was the picture of total relaxation, and Ann wondered if it was her imagination that made tension seem to hum around him.

"I found Becky sleeping in the alley behind this building. She'd been on the street for three or four days and she'd been alone for two weeks before that. She's a hell of a gritty kid."

Rafferty's mouth tightened at the recital of what Becky had been through. "I can't believe Maryanne would just leave her alone like that. She's just a baby."

"From the sounds of it, Becky was the more mature of the pair. I don't think your wife had a whole hell of a lot of common sense."

Rafferty stiffened and Ann held her breath. Flynn was deliberately trying to antagonize the man. Even if what he said was true, couldn't he have found a more tactful way to say it? Slowly, the tension eased from

Rafferty's broad shoulders. His mouth turned up in a rueful smile.

"I can't blame you for speaking your mind, Mc-Callister. You've done a lot for Becky, things I should have been there to do. I guess that gives you the right to ask a few questions.

"You're right. Maryanne didn't have much common sense."

Flynn set his coffee cup down and leaned forward, all pretense of relaxation gone. "What I'd really like to know is why your wife felt it necessary to take Becky and run away from you. I've had Becky in my care for over a month now and if you hadn't turned up, I was going to adopt her. The government may be satisfied with the fact that your name is on her birth certificate but, until *I'm* satisfied, Becky is staying right where she is."

The two men stared at each other, weighing and measuring in some way that Ann couldn't follow. Whatever he saw apparently decided Rafferty in Flynn's favor. He nodded slowly.

"I'd feel much the same in your position."

"Good. Then you wouldn't mind telling us why your wife took Becky and ran away."

"Maryanne was a very high strung, very sweet girl. And I use the word 'girl' deliberately. She just didn't seem to know how to grow up. I thought maybe she'd grow up when Becky was born but she didn't. She was a good mother but I'm not sure she ever really figured out that this wasn't a doll to play with. She'd dress the baby in fancy outfits with little ruffled hats and take her out in the stroller to show her off. When Becky was two, Maryanne bought matching mother and daughter outfits. They looked like something out of a magazine.''

He was silent for a moment, lost in memories. He shook himself, coming back to the present with an effort. ''I'm a doctor and my hours aren't all that regular. Maryanne wanted someone who could be there to pet and hold her, someone to take her out to dinner so she could show off her clothes. I wanted someone who understood how important my work was to me.''

He shrugged. ''It was a classic case of two people who didn't have enough in common. We quarreled a few times but never anything major. I wanted her to grow up and she wanted me to be a father figure. There was no middle ground.''

He reached for a coffee cup, turning it absently. His hands were huge and Ann had a hard time imagining them holding a scalpel or anything smaller than a tractor.

''Maryanne . . . did something that she thought was going to make me very angry. She was right. I was furious. But she'd been told that when I lost my temper, I was downright dangerous.'' He set the cup down, linking his hands together loosely, elbows braced on his thighs. ''I'll be the first to admit that I've got a nasty temper but I've yet to hit anybody, much less a woman. But she didn't know that and she thought . . . Hell, I don't know what she thought.''

His fingers tightened on each other until Ann was sure that knuckles would crack. ''We quarreled and I stormed out of the house. I went for a walk and ended up spending the night on a friend's sofa. I went straight to work from there. I figured we could both use the time to cool down. When I got home, she was gone and she'd taken Becky with her.

"I hired investigators but no one could turn up a trace of Maryanne or Becky. For all I knew, they were both dead, until I got the phone call from Ms. Davis."

He stopped speaking and no one else seemed inclined to say anything right away. Rafferty had told the story without fanfare or dramatics. He might have been talking about something that had nothing to do with him. But Ann had watched the way his fingers knotted over one another and she knew just how much it had cost him to dredge up the old memories. She looked at Flynn and could see that he was impressed despite himself.

"It's going to be awfully hard on Becky to just pack up and move. To her, you're a total stranger."

Rafferty nodded. "I know. She's just lost her mother. You two are the only security she knows right now. How did she take Maryanne's death?"

"Pretty well, I guess." Flynn took a swallow of coffee, his eyes on the cup. "I'm not sure she's completely grasped the reality of it. I think there's a part of her that still expects her mother to come back but we've done what we could to help her."

"Does she know how her mother died?"

"We decided to tell her that her mother fell and hit her head. Which, for all we know, is the truth. The coroner said that she died from a blow to the head but they don't know whether it was murder or an accident. She might have fallen accidentally and the guy she was with panicked and left her body in an aqueduct."

"Or he could have killed her." Rage rumbled in Rafferty's voice and Ann spoke quickly.

"We don't know that."

"And we never will." He thrust his fingers through his hair, tousling it into waves of gray. He gave her a quick, strained smile. "Don't worry. I'm not going to go hunting for this guy. There's nothing I can do for Maryanne. I've got to concentrate on Becky. I want to get to know my daughter again. You two know her a lot better than I do. What do you think would be the best way to tell her who I am?"

It was clearly not easy for him to ask for help, and Ann could not help but respect him for putting Becky's need above his own pride. She glanced at Flynn, but he appeared willing to let her take the lead.

"We thought that if Becky had a chance to get to know you before you leave, maybe even before she knows who you are, it might take a lot of the pressure off of her."

Rafferty stared at her for a long moment and then his eyes dropped to his hands. "You mean I should just hang around and let her get used to me and then tell her who I am? Seems like a hell of a way to get to know my own daughter, sneaking up on her?"

Flynn answered the pained question. "Becky's been through a lot lately. If we just drop it on her that her father has arrived, it's going to be pretty hard on her. You can stay here. There's plenty of room and it will give her a chance to get to know you without any pressure."

Rafferty ran his fingers through his hair and Ann held her breath, waiting for his decision. It couldn't be easy for him to rely on the advice of a pair of strangers for how to deal with his own child.

"Isn't she going to wonder why I'm staying here?"

"We can tell her that you're a friend of mine." Flynn's offer was made without expression, and Rafferty studied him for a long moment before nodding slowly.

"All right. I appreciate the offer."

Ann allowed herself to relax for the first time since hearing of Rafferty's existence.

"Now, I'd like to meet my daughter."

"I'll take you out and introduce you." They all stood up, but Ann caught Flynn's arm when he would have led Rafferty out to the balcony.

"I think Rafferty might appreciate a chance to meet Becky without an audience. She's out in the garden." She gestured to the sliding glass doors.

Rafferty gave her a grateful smile. "Thank you."

Flynn said nothing, but the muscles in his arm were rock hard beneath Ann's fingers as he watched the other man open the door and step out, sliding the glass shut behind him.

Chapter Ten

Rafferty threaded his way between wide planters, some overgrown with vegetation, some full of bare soil. The sun seemed stifling after the Indian summer he'd left in Colorado. He stopped next to a planter that contained a small jungle of ficus trees and unbuttoned his cuffs, rolling them up his forearms. It was a delaying tactic.

What was he going to say to Becky when he was finally face-to-face with her? How could he resist the need to pull her into his arms and hold her close? He had to remember that he was a total stranger to her, less welcome in her life than the two people in the penthouse behind him.

He walked on, feeling the rhythm of his pulse throbbing in his temples. Three years. Three years since he'd seen her. What would she look like? Did she look like her mother?

He came around the corner of a planter that contained a tangle of unidentifiable vegetation and stopped abruptly, feeling his heart almost stop also.

She was kneeling by a planter just a few feet away, digging in the bare soil with a small trowel, mounding the dirt carefully to one side. She was wearing bright

purple jeans and a purple-and-white striped top. Her
hair was pulled back in a ponytail, a bright yarn bow
slightly askew.

He swallowed hard, his hand going out for an instant before he jerked it back. He pushed both hands
in his back pockets to control the tremors that shook
them. He'd done surgery, knowing the patient's life
depended on the steadiness of his fingers, and his
hands had been rock steady. He drew in a quick
breath. He had to remember that he was supposed to
be nothing more than a friend of McCallister's.

"Hello, Becky." He hoped she wouldn't notice the
way his voice shook.

He moved forward as she turned to look at him and
Rafferty sank onto the edge of the planter, as much to
give himself support as anything else. The move put
his face almost level with hers.

"Hello. This roof belongs to Mr. Flynn, you know.
Did he say you could come out here?"

"I'm a friend of his."

She studied him for a long moment, her expression
solemn. Rafferty took the opportunity to study her,
his eyes devouring every inch of her. She'd changed so
much. The realization hurt. She wasn't the plump
toddler he remembered. This was a little girl on her
way to growing up. She was taller, of course. He'd
expected that. But he hadn't expected her to look so
different. She was slim, with none of the chubbiness
she'd had as a baby. And her eyes, her eyes looked so
much older and wiser than her years.

He felt a flash of anger. She'd had to grow up too
quickly. Maryanne had robbed her of part of her
childhood.

She looked like Maryanne. The same delicate features, elfin in a child, changing to beauty in a woman. But he could see himself in her face. The same stubborn chin, and her eyes weren't the pale blue of her mother's. Her eyes were gray, uncompromisingly gray.

"I guess If you're a friend of Mr. Flynn's, it's okay if you're out here."

Rafferty smiled, hoping she wouldn't notice that his eyes were too bright. "Thanks. I'm Rafferty."

"I'm Becky." She held out her hand and he took it.

The first time he'd been close enough to touch his daughter in three years. Her hand felt so tiny in his.

"I'm digging for gold."

He dragged his eyes from her face and looked at the hole she'd dug. "Have you had any luck?"

"Not yet but Mr. Flynn says you got to keep at something to make it work. And Ann says that pers...perst...."

"Persistence?"

"That's it. Ann says you got to have that to get anywhere."

"Sounds like you've had some pretty good advice."

"Mr. Flynn and Ann are my best friends in the whole world. They know everything."

Rafferty's mouth kicked up on one side. "Well, I hope you and I can be friends, too."

"We'll have to see if we like each other." Becky picked up the trowel and returned to her digging.

"I think we're going to like each other a lot, Becky."

He sat there, with the hot L.A. sun beating down and watched her dig in the soil. He'd missed so much of her life. Years that he could never regain. But he wouldn't miss any more of it.

IT WASN'T THAT he wasn't pleased for Becky's sake, but did Rafferty Traherne have to be so damned perfect?

Flynn picked up the dice and shook them before tossing them onto the table. A full house stared back at him. The fourth full house he'd had in a row. He stared at the Yahtzee score sheet, wondering what else he needed. Nothing that the dice were offering. He picked up the dice and threw them all again. At the end of his turn, he was forced to scratch his Yahtzee.

"You're not having much luck tonight, are you, Mr. Flynn?"

He smiled at Becky. "Not much. But you're making up for it, urchin. It's a good thing we're not gambling or I'd have lost the farm to you by now." She giggled.

Rafferty threw next and, of course, threw a Yahtzee on the second toss of the dice. Becky squealed with excitement and Ann laughed. Flynn smiled, but what he really wanted to do was throw the dice out the window.

No, if he was honest, what he really wanted to do was throw the man out the window.

No. He didn't want to do that. There was nothing wrong with Traherne. In fact, that was what was wrong with him. Couldn't the man have a few flaws? Bad breath. Bowlegs. Anything would do. But there was nothing.

He was absolutely perfect father material. He was patient with Becky but not above being firm. He had a good sense of humor; he was a polite house guest. He was good-looking, but not too good-looking. He probably loved God, America and apple pie, not necessarily in that order.

It was impossible not to like him but Flynn was trying.

He watched Ann smile across the table at Rafferty and felt a knot in his stomach that had nothing to do with the biscuits that Becky had made for dinner. Jealousy. Plain, old-fashioned jealousy. He was honest enough to admit that he felt it, but that didn't change the feelings.

In the last two weeks, Becky had come to adore Rafferty. Which was just as it should be. Flynn was doing what he could to loosen the ties between himself and Becky. It hurt but it had to be done. She needed to transfer her dependence to her father. He was glad that she was doing so.

He wasn't so glad that Ann seemed to think Rafferty was the greatest thing since sliced cheese. Did she have to smile at him quite so often?

He picked up the dice when his turn came and threw again, barely noticing when he had to put the results down on chance. His eyes caught Ann's as Rafferty picked up the dice. She gave him a flickering smile and then looked away, her fingers toying with her pencil.

She'd barely looked at him since Rafferty's arrival. In fact, come to think of it, they'd barely spoken since the night they made love. It seemed as if something was always taking priority. First there'd been the death of Becky's mother, then finding out about Rafferty and then Rafferty himself showing up.

Flynn wondered if he was the only one to feel the tension between them. There was so much left unspoken. Their relationship had taken a giant step and then been frozen in time. They couldn't go back to what they'd been before, but there was no saying what might lie in the future.

"Your turn, Flynn." He looked up, startled out of his thoughts. Ann was holding the dice out to him, her expression quizzical.

"Sorry. I guess I wasn't paying much attention." He reached out to take the dice from her, their fingers brushing. Their eyes met, and Flynn knew he wasn't the only one to feel the sparks that resulted from the casual contact.

Soon, he promised himself. Soon, they'd have time for each other.

"GOOD GAME. Not that the Raiders can compare to the Broncos, of course." Rafferty's grin took the sting out of the words.

Flynn lifted his hand, signaling for another round of beers before settling back in the booth and looking at his companion. "I haven't been to a football game in years."

"I thought you had season tickets." Rafferty emptied his mug as the waitress set another round down in front of them. He reached for his wallet, waving off Flynn's attempt to pay for them. "My treat. The tickets were yours."

"Thanks. But the tickets weren't exactly my treat. The family always has season seats. We just haven't used them in a while. My brother and I used to go almost every game."

"Did he switch to hockey?"

"He died and I guess I just got out of the habit." Flynn took a long swallow of the frosty beer, surprised by how little it hurt to mention Mark.

In the background, a country song twanged out the miseries of divorce. Two would-be cowboys played a desultory game of eight ball at a pool table near the jukebox. It was broad daylight outside but the bar was dusky, as if light never quite penetrated the shabby wooden walls. The bartender polished glasses with a rag that looked like it had been used to polish an engine.

"Must be tough, losing a brother. Was he younger or older?"

Flynn dragged his gaze away from the surroundings. "Older. Older and perfect. In fact, you remind me of Mark."

Rafferty raised an eyebrow, his skepticism clear. "I do? Doesn't seem likely. Perfect is hardly a word likely to be associated with me."

"Not perfect, maybe, but you're so damn upright. Mark was like that. It was impossible not to like him but it was hell living up to him."

"Upright? I don't know that I see myself that way."

"Sure you are. You're a doctor. You're a great father. You probably own your own home and I bet you contribute to an IRA every year."

Rafferty laughed. "Guilty. Are those the only criteria for being upright?"

"Just about."

"Then I guess I have to confess to the crime."

Flynn smiled. "It's not exactly a crime. What do you think of Becky?"

Rafferty's face softened, answering the question even before he spoke. "She's terrific."

"Yeah. I thought so myself."

"I'll be telling her who I am soon."

Flynn nodded. "I figured. I'm going to hate to lose her but there's no sense in dragging things out forever."

"I think..." Whatever Rafferty thought was destined to remain unspoken. While they were talking, Flynn had been vaguely aware that the bar was filling up. Urban cowboys, construction workers and an assortment of women, accompanied and otherwise. The jukebox had been turned up and one or two couples were rocking back and forth on a tiny strip of space that could optimistically be called a dance floor.

It was the dance floor that was the source of the sudden trouble. Apparently, three men were claiming the privilege of the same dance with one woman. The disagreement had escalated into a shouting match. It was only a moment before the first punch was thrown.

Rafferty and Flynn slid out of the booth, both of them with the same thought in mind. To slip quietly and unobtrusively out of the bar. Unfortunately, things were not destined to work out quite that neatly. The fighting in the middle of the room seemed to have a ripple effect. Every man in the place remembered a grudge against the man next to him. Before they'd gone more than three steps from their booth, they were involved in a full-fledged brawl.

Flynn ducked under a punch thrown at him by a man in a cowboy hat and buried his left fist in the man's overfed belly, coming up with his right fist against the cowboy's chin. The man staggered back and Flynn spun to check Rafferty's progress. Rafferty was holding his own, using his sheer bulk to force his way toward the door and using his fists when he had to.

A journey that had taken a matter of seconds earlier in the day took closer to ten minutes in the midst of the brawl. Flynn could feel the adrenaline pounding in his temples as he ducked flying fists and flying

bottles, always keeping the door in sight. He jumped
forward, pulling a man off Rafferty's back and spinning him into the melee around them. Rafferty turned.

"Thanks."

"Don't mention it." Rafferty's eyes went past him,
widening. Flynn spun around. He caught only a
glimpse of a stop-sign red shirt, a black beard and an
upraised hand. He threw up his arm. The bottle that
would have landed on his head and removed half his
face, shattered against his forearm instead. He was
aware of pain but there was no time to worry about it
now. Rafferty came around him like a freight train.
Red-shirt didn't have time to react and Flynn saw the
startled look on his face as Rafferty's fist connected
with his chin, rocking him back on his heels. A second blow sent him crashing to the floor.

Rafferty turned, his eyes bright. "You okay?" He
had to shout to be heard. Flynn nodded. "Let's get the
hell out of here."

They were only a few feet from the door, and seconds later they ducked through into the relative quiet
of the street. Both men collapsed back against the
building. Inside the battle raged on, shouts and ob-
scenities mixing with the shatter of breaking glass.

Flynn rolled his head to look at Rafferty, their eyes
meeting in the dusky light. They were both disheveled. Rafferty's lip was split and oozing blood sullenly. His jacket had been left behind in the bar, his
shirt was torn and his jeans were covered with beer.
Flynn knew he looked at least as bad. He could feel
blood soaking the fabric of his shirt. He had no idea
how bad the cut was. He only hoped he wasn't bleeding to death. Every muscle in his body ached.

He grinned, feeling more alive than he'd felt in years. "Hell of a fight."

Rafferty grinned back, wincing as the gesture tugged at his split lip. "Hell of a fight." He dabbed at the blood on his chin. "How bad is your arm?"

Flynn shrugged, still grinning. "I have no idea."

"Ought to check it out." The wail of sirens punctuated his remark and their eyes met again. "We'll check it out later."

Flynn nodded. "I can't imagine Ann's reaction if I had to call and ask her to bail us out of jail."

"Think we can make it to the car before the cops get here?"

"We can try." Flynn pushed himself away from the wall and sprinted the half block to the Ferrari, aware of Rafferty right behind him. They arrived at the car just as the first squad cars came around the corner ahead of them. Flynn skidded to a halt by the passenger door, tossing the keys to Rafferty.

"You drive. I don't think my arm is up to it."

Rafferty walked around the end of the car, glancing up as if mildly curious when the police cars hurried by, lights and sirens going. He opened the car door and slid inside, flicking open the lock for Flynn. Flynn slipped into the dark interior and shut the door.

"Wonder where they're going."

"I have no idea." Their eyes met and they both grinned like a couple of teenagers. Their friendship was cemented in those moments.

An hour later, Flynn turned the key in the apartment door. "Ann's not going to be happy."

"We could lie and tell her we were rescuing someone from a fate worse than death."

"Just what is a fate worse than death?"

Rafferty shrugged his huge shoulders. "I don't know."

Flynn hesitated, the key still in the lock. "She'd never believe it."

He withdrew the key and opened the door. Inside, a peculiar acrid smell assaulted their noses, and Flynn stopped dead just inside the hall.

"Becky's cooking again."

Rafferty had had some experience with his daughter's cooking and he winced, both at the smell and at the thought of what might have caused it. "I wonder what's she's made."

"I don't want to know."

"Me neither. Let's go back to the bar. It's probably safer."

Flynn grinned at Rafferty's suggestion. He pushed the door shut behind them but he didn't take off his coat. The black leather served to conceal the blood that soaked his arm. With luck, he could get into the bathroom and deal with the wound without Becky or Ann being any the wiser. If it needed medical attention, he could call on Rafferty's expertise.

"Hi, Mr. Flynn. Hi, Rafferty. I'm making a cake." Becky greeted them as they stepped into the living room. Her small form was swathed in an apron, but it hadn't prevented flour from coating every exposed surface. "Did you have fun?"

"We had a lot of fun, pumpkin." Rafferty came around Flynn and scooped Becky, dropping a kiss on her flour-dusted hair. "What kind of cake are you making?"

"Spice. Ann says she thinks I may have added too much cinnamon."

Flynn inhaled, finally identifying the acrid scent as burning spices. He had the feeling that Ann was right. Ann came out of the kitchen, also apron-wrapped. She had flour in her hair and a slightly harried expression on her face, and Flynn thought she'd never looked more beautiful.

"How was your..." Her eyes, more critical than Becky's, went over the two of them, seeing the bruise starting to show on Rafferty's cheekbone, his swollen lip and torn shirt, Flynn's disheveled hair and clothes and the careful way he held his left arm.

"What happened?"

"Nothing. We stopped and had a drink after the game."

"A drink? That's all?"

Rafferty looked from Ann to Flynn and took hold of Becky's hand. "How would you like to go to a movie?"

"Yeah!"

"Coward." He shrugged without apology in answer to Flynn's quiet accusation.

"Sorry. I don't think it's good for Becky to see bloodshed and I have a feeling that's what's about to occur."

"Who's going to blood?"

"Bleed, sweetheart. Nobody's going to bleed. I was just kidding. Why don't you come help me find a new shirt and we'll go out to the movies."

"Is Mr. Flynn and Ann going to come, too?"

Becky's ungrammatical question was the last sentence spoken until she and Rafferty returned a moment later. Rafferty was shrugging into a clean shirt. Becky was carrying a jacket.

"Okay if I borrow a car?"

"If it wasn't for Becky, I'd make you walk to the theater. Take the Ferrari. I just hope you can sleep tonight after abandoning a friend in need."

Rafferty grinned, not in the least disturbed by Flynn's dark warning. "Ann's too nice to do more than minor damage." He looked at Ann's set face. "It really wasn't our fault."

The door shut, leaving Ann and Flynn in the quiet apartment.

"What happened?"

Flynn shrugged, wincing as the gesture shifted his arm. "Nothing much. A little fight broke out in the bar and we got involved in the edges of it while we were trying to get to the door."

"How badly are you hurt?"

"Not bad. A few scrapes and bruises. It really wasn't that bad a fight."

"Then why are you favoring your arm?" She was wearing a pink apron that clashed with the fiery red of her hair, her feet were encased in bright blue socks and he knew exactly how her jeans molded her firm body. She looked absolutely feminine, except for the stern line of her mouth.

Flynn didn't want to talk about his arm, or the fight. He didn't want to talk about Rafferty or Becky or the fact that soon they'd be going away and he'd be alone again. He wanted to pull Ann into his arms and kiss the stern expression from her face. He wanted to feel her soften against him.

"Do you realize this is the first time we've been alone in a month?"

Awareness flickered through her eyes for a moment before being sternly pushed aside. "Let me see your arm."

"It's really not that big a deal."

"Then you won't mind me taking a look at it, will you?"

To tell the truth, his arm was beginning to throb like the devil. Besides, if he wanted to seduce Ann, it would be nice if he weren't bleeding all over her.

"All right. I would appreciate it if you took a look at it. To tell the truth, I haven't looked at it since it happened."

If she was suspicious of his abrupt capitulation, he couldn't tell it from her expression. He led the way into the huge bathroom off his bedroom and then stood there, looking as helpless as possible. All was fair in love and war. He wasn't quite ready to call this one or the other. All he knew was that he wanted Ann in his bed again and, if he could accomplish that by playing on her sympathies, then he wasn't above doing that.

Ann pulled a wicker stool over next to the sink. "Sit down and we'll see if we can get that coat off."

He sat down and shrugged the coat off his uninjured arm, letting Ann ease it off the other arm. He didn't have to pretend to a pained silence when the fabric stuck to the wound. In fact, by the time Ann was through fixing him up, he felt worse than he had before she started.

She took one look at the cut and announced that it would require stitches. Flynn's protests were ignored as she fetched her medical bag and proceeded to scrub the wound with what he would have sworn was pure lye. She stitched the arm without local anesthetic, announcing that he was big enough to handle the pain. Flynn thought of suggesting that he might prefer not to handle the pain, but her disapproval was so palpable that he decided not to risk her ire any further.

As it turned out, she wielded the needle so carefully that he barely felt the four stitches she put in his arm. He watched her as she worked, her head bent over him, her attention on the job at hand.

"There. That should do it." She picked up a roll of gauze and began to wind it around his arm. "If you can just stay out of barroom brawls for a while and give it a chance to heal."

"I'll see what I can do." He lifted his free hand and tugged loose the pins holding her hair.

"Don't." But her protest came too late. His nimble fingers found the last pin and her hair tumbled onto her shoulders. She tried to ignore him, concentrating on taping the gauze bandage shut. But it was hard to ignore the way his fingers burrowed into her hair, finding the tense muscles at the back of her neck.

"You're too tense. You should relax more."

"Flynn..." She tried to back away but his hand tightened, pulling her closer. Seated on the wicker stool, his eyes were just level with hers, but she didn't want to meet his eyes. "Let me go."

"Look at me." He was so close that his breath stirred the hair that curled against her temples. Slowly, her eyes came up to meet his and she felt her knees weaken. It wasn't fair. How could his eyes be so blue, so full of need?

"Flynn..." He stilled her whispered protest with a quick kiss, stealing away her voice.

"Stay with me tonight."

"I can't. I..." He kissed her again and she forgot what she'd planned to say.

"Stay with me. I just want to hold you."

She started to shake her head but his mouth stopped the movement. The kiss was longer this time. His mouth molded hers, stealing not only her breath, but the ability to think.

"Please, Ann. I want you with me tonight."

"Flynn..." She wasn't quite sure how they'd gotten from the bathroom to the bedroom. Sometime during that drugging kiss, he must have eased her in here. She didn't remember walking but he certainly hadn't carried her. He kissed her again, his fingers untying the frilly apron.

"We can just sleep. I won't push you into anything more." He tugged the apron off and his attention moved to the buttons on her cotton shirt. For a man with full use of only one hand, he didn't seem to be having any trouble getting her clothes off.

Before Ann could marshall her thoughts, she was standing in front of him clad in a lacy camisole and tap pants, not quite sure how she'd come to be there. He reached around her to turn down the covers on the bed.

She hesitated, aware that this was a crossroads in some way that she couldn't quite define. Once in that bed, she would have taken a step toward... Toward what? She wasn't sure, but she knew it would change her life.

Flynn unsnapped his jeans and then waited. He could feel Ann's hesitation and he held his breath. He wouldn't pressure her but, if she walked away now, he felt as if something inside him would die. She looked up at him, her eyes bright green with questions he couldn't read, and then she turned and slid onto the bed.

He released his breath in a rush, unzipping his jeans and slipping them off. He left his briefs on as he climbed into bed beside her. He'd said that he just wanted to hold her and that was all he'd ask of her.

He reached out, pulling her close. Ann snuggled against his side, her small body seeming made to fit his, her head resting on his shoulder. Flynn reached up to shut out the light, plunging the room into darkness.

He rested his cheek against her hair, feeling complete for the first time in a very long time.

Chapter Eleven

Flynn came awake slowly, aware of feeling completely rested. He'd slept heavily but he didn't feel groggy. He didn't have to open his eyes to know the source of his contentment. Ann was snuggled against his side, one arm thrown over his chest, one leg nestled intimately across his thighs.

He kissed her forehead, brushing aside a bright curl to find the soft skin beneath. She stirred, tipping her head back. He didn't know if the invitation was deliberate or not, but he wasn't going to turn it down. He kissed his way down her face, planting soft kisses at the corners of her eyes, on the tip of her nose, on the delicate skin just under her jaw.

She stirred again and he knew she was awake. His lips teased the corners of her mouth and her lips parted, inviting him. His mouth settled over hers. It was a sleepy kiss, warm with passion that didn't need to be rushed.

Flynn's hand slid up her side, beneath the hem of her camisole, finding sleep-warmed skin that heated to his touch. Ann moaned against his mouth as his hand cupped her breast, testing its weight, finding the soft peak that hardened with the stroke of his thumb.

Still without speaking, Flynn shifted her until she lay on top of him, her breasts pressed against his chest with only the thin silk between them, her thighs lying between his. He brought his knees up, cradling her.

His hands burrowed into the thickness of her hair, pulling her face to his. The sleepy passion took on an edge of urgency. The kiss was a little harder, a little more demanding, and Ann met him with demands of her own.

His hands tugged impatiently at the camisole and she lifted herself so that he could tug the garment over her head. His hands caught her around the rib cage, lifting her higher, sliding her up his body. He heard her pleasure as his mouth closed around her nipple, stroking the pale pink tip to hardness. He held her helpless, suspended in his hands while he took his pleasure of her. He took his time, painting each breast with tongue strokes, covering every inch of soft flesh, feeling her desire in his hands.

He lowered her slowly, reluctant to give up the tender territory he'd conquered but needing the taste of her mouth. The kiss was explosive, the impact of it rolling through both of them. Suddenly, all the patience was gone. His hands fought the silk tap pants, hearing the fine silk tear but not caring. All that mattered was that her skin be bare to his touch. He couldn't stand anything that kept him away from her.

She struggled with the stretchy fabric of his briefs, her breath leaving her in a frustrated sigh when her hands couldn't master the task. Flynn brushed her hands aside and suddenly there was nothing between them. He rolled, putting her beneath him. Her legs parted, cradling him. His mouth caught hers, his tongue plunged inside at the same moment that he sheathed his aching hardness in the damp warmth of her body.

Flynn swallowed the keening moan that left her throat. The emptiness was filled, but the hunger was still there. He moved, feeling her body shift to accommodate his, tasting the response she gave so willingly.

He wanted to drag the moment out forever. But the need was too strong, the hunger too long denied. Ann shivered beneath him, her body contracting around him, and Flynn groaned, following her to the culmination of their passionate love.

Not a word had been spoken, but they communicated as fully as was humanly possible.

RAFFERTY WOKE SUDDENLY, aware that he was no longer alone. He was lying on his stomach, his face near the edge of the bed. He opened his eyes to find Becky seated on the floor next to the bed. She was still in her pajamas. Clutched in her arms was the tattered brown giraffe he'd given her for her second birthday. Her eyes were wide and solemn on his face.

"Good morning." He blinked, clearing the last remnants of sleep from his eyes. He rolled onto his back and pulled himself up until he could lean against the headboard. A glance at the clock told him it was barely six o'clock.

"You're up early. Did you have a bad dream?"

"No." She continued to stare at him and Rafferty's eyes narrowed, studying the intent expression on her face.

"What is it, Becky? Is something bothering you?"

"Are you my daddy?" The question was so totally unexpected that Rafferty had a moment of wondering if he was still asleep and dreaming this confrontation. But, looking at Becky's serious little face, he knew this was no dream.

"Would you like it if I was your daddy?"

She shrugged, her eyes dropping from his face. Her fingers twisted an ear on the battered stuffed toy. "I don't know. I guess it would be okay." She stopped but Rafferty didn't say anything. He knew there was more.

"If you're my daddy, how come you left me and Mama? How come you left us?"

He chose his words carefully, knowing that what he said now could affect their relationship for a very long time to come. "Your mother and I had an argument a long time ago. She thought I was very angry with her and she thought I was going to stay angry forever. So, she took you and she left."

"Were you mad?"

"I . . . was angry for a little while but I got over it. Your mother just didn't realize that I'd get over it. After she left, I looked for the two of you but I couldn't find you. I never stopped looking, Becky."

He waited a long time, hardly breathing. Had he said the right things? Was there something more he should have told her, some other way to say it?

"Did your mother ever talk about me?" It was taking a chance to ask the question, but he had to know what Maryanne had told her.

She shrugged without looking at him. "It always made her cry when I asked about you."

He closed his eyes, and for an instant, it was as if Maryanne was standing in front of him. She'd been such a sweet pretty girl. It wasn't her fault that she just hadn't known how to grow up. Yes, he could imagine that she'd cried when Becky asked about him. He'd never doubted that, in her own way, she'd loved him.

"We used to have a lot of fun together when you were little. You probably don't remember much of that."

Her eyes flickered up at him and then away. "I remember you used to throw me up in the air. And sometimes you'd tell me a bedtime story. Only you'd read it out of a book. You didn't make one up like Mr. Flynn does. Mama had a picture of you that she'd show me sometimes only your hair was all streaky. Not one color like it is now."

Rafferty ran his fingers through his iron-gray hair. "When your mother left, my hair hadn't gone completely gray yet. It runs in my family, you know. Your grandfather's hair was gray by the time he was thirty."

"Grandfather? Do I have a grandfather?"

"Sure. And a grandmother, too. And you've got two aunts and three cousins."

Her eyes widened at this bounty of relatives. "All those?"

"All those. That is, if you want me to be your dad."

She stared at him for a long time. "I think I'd like that."

Rafferty blinked, swallowing the hard knot in his throat. If his smile was shaky around the edges, he didn't think she'd care. He reached out one hand, careful not to expect too much too soon. Becky stood up and reached out to take his hand, her small fingers engulfed in his huge palm. She hesitated a moment, as if weighing him in some balance in her mind, and then she threw herself forward.

Rafferty's arms closed around her and he buried his face in her sandy hair. She smelled of soap and baby powder. His chest ached as her arms went around his neck.

He'd lost so much time with her. Three years gone never to be regained. He'd never lose sight of how lucky he was to have her back with him.

IT WAS AFTER NINE when all the inhabitants of the penthouse met up. Rafferty and Becky were in the kitchen cooking pancakes when Ann and Flynn showed up. Rafferty had his own theories as to who had slept where the night before, which was why he hadn't let Becky wake Flynn to announce that she'd found her father. When Flynn wandered into the kitchen, Becky pounced on him.

"Guess what, Mr. Flynn. Guess what."

"It's too early to guess anything, urchin. Are you helping Rafferty cook breakfast?" He eyed the pancakes cautiously. Rafferty grinned and waved the spatula.

"Becky is only supervising this morning."

"That's nice. Now, what is it I'm supposed to guess?"

He sank into a chair, leaning his elbow on the kitchen table, his expression indulgent as Becky hopped up and down in front of him.

"Rafferty is my dad. My real live dad. He and Mama had a fight and she left but he never stopped looking for us. Isn't that neat?"

Flynn's smile was twisted as he reached out to ruffle her hair. There was a sharp pain in his chest as he looked at her. Just in the few weeks he'd known her, she'd grown so much. It hurt to think that he wouldn't be there to watch her grow and see her change.

"That's great, Becky. I'm really happy for you."

Rafferty flipped a pancake and then leaned one leg against the counter. "I've got reservations on a flight back to Denver late this afternoon."

"So soon?" The protest came from Ann who'd come to stand in the doorway. It was clear that she'd heard Becky's news. Her eyes shimmered with quick tears, and Flynn had to resist the urge to go to her and put his arms around her. It wasn't as if they hadn't known that this moment was coming. It was just that it was difficult to let go now that the time had come.

Ann looked from Becky to Rafferty. He shook his head, his eyes understanding.

"I don't see any sense in dragging things out. Goodbyes are best said quickly."

"You're right, of course." Ann blinked, clearing her eyes. The smile she gave Becky shook around the edges but not enough for Becky to notice.

"I'm really excited for you, Becky. I know you're going to love living with your dad."

"Yeah. He says there's snow and everything." Clearly, the 'everything' wasn't nearly as interesting as the snow.

"Denver isn't that far away. You guys should come visit us this winter. We'll go to Aspen for the skiing."

"Sure we will." Flynn looked at Ann, wondering if she'd noticed the way Rafferty automatically paired them. Wondering what she was thinking.

No MATTER HOW QUICKLY SAID, the goodbyes were still painful. Becky had been part of Flynn's life a relatively short time, but she'd wound herself deep into his emotions. It wasn't easy to say goodbye.

Rafferty refused Flynn's offer of a ride to the airport. A taxi was expensive, but it would save them all a painful parting in public.

"You've got Frankie, don't you?" It was the second time Ann had asked the question, but Becky answered it again.

"He's in Daddy's purse."

Rafferty winced. "Carry-on luggage, pumpkin, not a purse." Ann smiled but her mouth shook and she had to bite her lip, half turning away until she controlled her expression.

"Don't cry, Ann. You and Mr. Flynn will come see us soon, won't you?"

"You bet we will, urchin." Flynn crouched next to the little girl, his eyes going over her face. "You take care of your dad, okay? And don't go getting lost in any snowbanks." He ruffled her hair, keeping his smile tacked in place. He stood up and held out his hand to Rafferty. "Take care of her. She's a pretty special kid."

"I will." Rafferty shook hands with Flynn and then took Ann's hand, pulling her close to brush a kiss over her cheek. "Come and see us soon."

"We will." Ann's smile was shaky but intact and she bent to hug Becky. "See you later, Becky."

"Okay. Say goodbye to Oscar for me."

"I will."

Flynn leaned against the edge of the door as they walked to the elevators. Behind him, Ann swallowed a sob. His chest ached as the elevator door slid open. Rafferty stepped in but Becky hesitated. She turned around and Flynn smiled, lifting his hand in a casual wave. She stared at him for a long minute and then tugged her hand loose from her father's and ran back.

Flynn dropped to one knee, catching her as she flew toward him, burying his face in her hair, breathing in all the sweet little girl smells that he'd grown to love.

"I love you, Mr. Flynn." It was as if she'd only just realized that she was really leaving him behind.

"I love you too, Becky." His voice broke on the words and he held her tighter. They stayed that way for the space of several slow heartbeats and then Flynn drew back. He smiled at Becky, reaching up to brush a tear from her cheek.

"I'll come and visit you soon. I promise."

"Will you tell me a story before I go to bed?"

"You bet. But I bet your dad tells a pretty mean story himself." Becky looked over her shoulder at Rafferty, who was standing just outside the open elevator. She looked back at Flynn, torn between the excitement of a father and the security Flynn represented.

"Go on. You're going to miss your flight and then the two of you will have to walk all the way to Colorado."

He turned her around and gave her a gentle push toward Rafferty. She took two steps and then hesitated, looking back at him. He smiled, hoping she wouldn't notice the unnatural brightness of his eyes.

"Scoot, urchin." She looked at him a moment longer, her gray eyes full of uncertainty and then turned and ran to her father. Rafferty caught her hand in his and stepped into the elevator. Flynn stood up, watching as the elevator doors slid shut, closing Becky from sight.

He shoved his hands in his back pockets, staring at the blank panels for a long time, blinking rapidly against the burning in his eyes. Behind him, Ann sobbed quietly.

He turned at last to find her leaning against the wall, her eyes brimming over, one fist pressed to her mouth as if to hold back the sobs. He put his arm around her shoulders, leading her back into the apartment and shutting the door.

"Come on. It isn't like we'll never see her again."

"I know."

"And it isn't as if she wasn't going to have a good home."

"I know." She let him lead her to the sofa and settle them both onto the soft cushions.

"Rafferty is a terrific guy."

"I know."

"So why are you crying?"

"I'm going to miss her so much." The words came out on a hiccoughed sob and Flynn's heart twisted.

"I know, love." He pulled her head to his shoulder and Ann collapsed against him, one hand curling around the edge of his shirt. "Go ahead and cry."

She cried for a long time, crying out her grief over losing Becky, but also crying out the confusion that seemed to have taken over her life. Nothing fit into the neat patterns she'd devised for herself. Most of all, Flynn McCallister didn't fit into any pattern.

When she lay still against him, he brushed the tangled hair back from her face. He dropped a kiss on her flushed forehead, tilting her face back to place another kiss on her still trembling mouth.

"I must look awful." It was a measure of her exhaustion that she didn't try to hide her tear-streaked face.

"Actually, you do look pretty terrible." Ann's eyes flew open in shock.

"What?"

"I said you look pretty terrible. Your eyes are red, your nose is red, your face is red. Actually, now that I think about it, your hair is red, too, so you look kind of coordinated. Everything matches. Think you could do it in purple?"

Despite herself, Ann laughed, which was exactly what he'd been trying for. He ducked the pillow she swung at him.

"Fiend."

"*Moi?* I was simply agreeing with you. My mother always told me to agree with a lady." His face was the very picture of injured innocence and Ann laughed again.

"What am I going to do with you?"

"I could think of several possibilities." He waggled his eyebrows in a lascivious manner. She chuckled again but it died out on a sigh.

"I really am going to miss her."

"I know. I am, too." She settled back onto his shoulder, and he wondered if the position felt as right to her as it did to him.

"I've never spent much time around children. I wonder if they're all as neat as Becky."

"I doubt it, but Becky does tend to put parenthood in a new perspective."

"Yeah." Ann sighed.

They sat in silence for a long time, staring at the empty fireplace, their thoughts drifting. The grandfather clock chimed and Flynn cocked his head, counting each mellow bong.

"Six o'clock. Their plane left fifteen minutes ago."

There was another long silence. Flynn suddenly sat up, dislodging Ann from her comfortable position.

"Where are you going?"

"There's no sense in sitting here moping all night." He stood up as Ann pulled herself upright on the sofa, tugging her shirt back into place.

"You're right. Becky is happy. We should be happy for her. I guess I'll go home. Oscar probably thinks I've died."

Flynn felt a surge of panic. She couldn't go home. Not now. Not yet. He had the feeling that, if she went home now, they might never find each other again. Ridiculous, of course, but he never argued with a gut feeling. Becky had been the tie that bound them together. Now Becky was gone. Did they have anything left?

"Dinner."

Ann looked up at him, startled by the way the word came at her so forcefully. "Dinner?"

"Dinner." He smiled crookedly, bowing low. "I would consider myself honored if you would dine with me this evening."

"Like this?" She pushed her tangled hair back and stood up, looking down at her jeans and shirt. "I look like I've been dragged through a knothole backward."

"How about if we meet in the hallway at eight. I know a great restaurant where the lobster is slathered in butter. I'll call and see if I can get reservations."

TWO HOURS LATER, Ann stepped nervously out of her apartment. She felt like a sixteen-year-old going out on her first date. It had been years since she'd spent so much time fussing with her appearance. She'd tried on every garment in her closet, finally setting on an emerald-green silk sheath and matching silk pumps that added inches to her height. She'd brushed her hair ruthlessly, finally pinning it into a soft Gibson girl style, leaving tendrils loose to caress her neck.

The time she'd spent was immediately forgotten when she saw the look in Flynn's eyes. He'd been waiting for her, leaning bonelessly against the wall. He straightened as she stepped through the door. Ann froze, feeling the butterflies in her stomach jump nervously. His eyes went over her, starting at the top of her head and working their way down to her elegantly shod feet and then reversing the journey.

When his eyes finally stopped on her face, Ann felt her toes curl inside the narrow pumps. He was looking at her as if she were the most exquisite thing he'd ever seen. The blue of his eyes seemed to penetrate deep into her soul, leaving her weak and trembling.

They stared at each other without speaking for a long, still moment. At last, Flynn walked toward her, his stride deliberate, his eyes never leaving her face. He stopped in front of her and Ann looked up at him. The dark suit made his shoulders seem wider than ever. Caught between his bulk and the thick door at her back, she felt vulnerable, deliciously feminine, excited and scared at the same time.

"You are so beautiful."

He reached for her hand, lifting it to his mouth, but turning it at the last minute so that his kiss landed in her palm. His mouth felt warm and dry against her skin and then his teeth closed over the fleshy area at the base of her thumb, nipping gently, sending a shiver up her arm. Ann closed her eyes, leaning back against the door when her knees threatened to give way.

His lips touched lightly on the inside of her wrist, and then he placed her hand in the crook of his arm. She opened her eyes, wondering if she looked as dazed as she felt.

"Your carriage awaits, madam."

The Ferrari wasn't quite a carriage, but it served just as well. Closed in the intimate interior, they might have been alone in the world. They didn't speak much on the way to the restaurant. There didn't seem to be any need.

The evening seemed to have a fairy-tale quality to it. The table was tucked in a dimly lit corner. The service was exquisitely unobtrusive; the food was beautifully prepared. The wine was smooth, slipping over the tongue like warm velvet. And Flynn's eyes couldn't seem to get enough of her.

Never had Ann felt so cherished, so wanted. He made her feel as if she were the only person in the room. They talked about impersonal things: food, wine, books and movies. He listened carefully to her opinion on the least of subjects, making her feel that what she had to say was important to him. It was an amazingly seductive feeling.

Ann ordered medallions of beef and Flynn ordered the lobster. When the meals arrived, he caught her looking longingly at his plate.

"You should have ordered the lobster."

Ann cut into her beef, finding it meltingly tender. "It's impossible to eat lobster neatly and I don't want to end the evening with butter on my chest." She took a bite of beef and then looked up to find Flynn's eyes on the décolletage of her dress.

"I'm sure I could think of some way to get it off." His eyes swept up to hers, and Ann forgot how to chew when she saw the hunger he made no attempt to conceal. She was grateful when he looked away. She swallowed without having the slightest idea what she'd just tasted.

Flynn concentrated on his lobster, giving her a chance to slow her pulse. But it picked up again when he dipped a bite of his entrée in butter and held it across the table to her.

"You can't possibly get butter on your dress this way."

Feeling self-conscious, Ann leaned forward and took the proffered tidbit. Her teeth sank into the succulent white flesh and she closed her eyes in ecstasy, savoring the buttery richness of it. When she opened her eyes, she found Flynn staring at her. The need there made her feel like a siren. Her eyes never leaving his face, she let her tongue come out, licking the butter off her lips with slow deliberation.

Flynn's eyes blazed electric blue, making her wonder if she was starting something she wasn't going to be able to finish. She looked away, reaching for her water glass, though it was going to take more than water to quench the fire they were starting.

"I should have brought the Mercedes."

"Why?"

"Because then I wouldn't have to wait until we got home to make love to you."

The water glass hit the table with a thump as her eyes flew to his face. "What?"

"You heard me. As it is, we'll have to wait till we get home. I'm a little old for the contortions the Ferrari would require. But once I get you home, I'm going to strip that sexy dress off of you an inch at a time and

I'm going to taste every single inch until you beg me to make love to you.''

His tone was conversational, almost casual, and Ann wondered if she was hearing things. Then she saw the look in his eyes and knew that she hadn't dreamed the things he'd just said. She could feel the color start at her toes and creep over her body like a slow red tide until it reached her face. She stared at him a moment longer, and then her eyes dropped away and she busied herself with her meal.

There was silence for a few minutes and then she looked up again, her eyes mischievous. ''Are you sure you're too old for the Ferrari?''

His expression promised retribution of the sweetest kind.

Though she knew the food was exquisite, Ann couldn't really say that she tasted much of it. All her attention was for the man across from her. They said very little during the meal, but she could feel the tension building to a boiling point.

They both refused dessert and Flynn paid the bill. He put his hand against the small of her back as they walked from the restaurant, and Ann wondered if the sparks that seemed to shoot from that light touch were visible to the other patrons.

They didn't speak as they waited for the elevator to arrive. Another couple got off and Flynn nodded politely to them as he ushered Ann into the luxurious cubicle. He pushed the button to take them to the parking garage and the doors slid silently shut.

In an instant, Ann found herself pinned to the wall, Flynn's body a heavy weight against her. Startled, she looked up but she caught only a glimpse of his eyes, dark with passion; then his mouth came down on hers.

She melted instantly, her body flowing into his, her arms snaking around his neck.

She forgot where they were, forgot who she was, forgot everything but the feel of his mouth on hers, the scent of Aramis tickling her nose. She moaned a protest when Flynn eased his mouth away. Her lashes felt weighted as she opened her eyes.

"The elevator has stopped." It took a minute for the words to sink in. She looked around, still dazed.

"Elevator?"

Flynn's grin was pure masculinity. He wrapped an arm around her shoulders and led her out of the elevator and to the Ferrari, tucking her into the seat as if she were the rarest of treasures.

Neither of them said a word on the drive home. The tension inside the low-slung sports car was so thick, it seemed to be almost breathable. He pulled the car into his parking space, his movement controlled. Ann could feel every breath she took as they walked to the elevator, not touching, not speaking. The doors closed behind them and she was in his arms, their bodies melding hungrily.

Ann didn't notice when the doors slid open on their floor. She wouldn't have noticed if the doors had slid open on Wilshire Boulevard. Flynn bent without taking his mouth from hers, his arm catching her behind the knees, lifting her off her feet and into his arms. Ann's fingers worked their way into the thick blackness of his hair as he carried her to his apartment, kicking the door shut behind them.

He carried her through the silent rooms to his bedroom, laying her on the bed and following her down, pinning her with the sensual weight of his body.

She couldn't have said if it was hours or days later when they at last fell asleep. She was conscious of nothing beyond the warmth of Flynn lying next to her, his ragged breathing slowly steadying. He'd kept every promise he'd made her in the restaurant.

Chapter Twelve

When Ann awoke the next morning, she knew immediately that she was alone. She rolled over in the huge bed, burying her face in Flynn's pillow and breathing in the mixture of scents that she knew she would always associate with him.

She opened her eyes and sat up, feeling more alive than she had ever felt before. She cocked her head, listening, but the apartment was quiet. With a shrug, she swung her legs out of bed. She had to be at the hospital in an hour. It was probably just as well that Flynn was gone.

Her clothes were neatly folded and stacked on a chair and she flushed, remembering how quickly they'd been discarded the night before. Lying on top of her silk slip with a folded piece of paper. She picked it up, feeling as quivery as a school girl.

Ann,
Sorry I'm not there to kiss you awake but I'd probably end up making you late for work. I had to go out to my parents'. Some papers Dad needs me to sign. Let's have dinner again tonight. Maybe, this time, I'll manage to taste some of the

food. I'll pick you up at eight. Wear the green
dress again. I had such fun peeling it off of you.

Love, Flynn

Ann hugged the note to her chest, her cheeks pink
with the memory of their lovemaking the night before. Her smile widened. She might have waited a long
time to take a lover, but she'd certainly picked a win-
ner. She threw on a robe of Flynn's and gathered up
her clothes before hurrying to her own apartment.
There would be time for basking in a rosy glow later.
Right now, she had to get to work.

But, as the day wore on, some of the glow faded to
be replaced by a host of uncertainties. What was she
getting into? Never in her wildest dreams could she
have imagined that she would be attracted to a man
like Flynn McCallister. He was exciting and she'd certainly learned that he had a warm side, which she'd
never have expected. But he seemed to drift through
life without any real thoughts of the future. She
sometimes wondered if he ever thought of tomorrow
at all.

Yes, he'd been wonderful with Becky, but there was
more to life than being kind to small children and animals. There was dedication and ambition and... Well,
weren't dedication and ambition important enough?
And he didn't have a trace of either one.

And what was it that he wanted from her? Was he
looking for a brief affair? A long-term affair? He
couldn't be thinking in terms of marriage, could he?
Because she certainly wasn't thinking in those terms.
Flynn was the dreamer. Ann Perry was a very practical woman who knew better than to think that love
alone could support a marriage.

Love?

A slip of the thought. She wasn't in love with him. Or was she?

By the time eight o'clock rolled around, Ann had argued with herself until her stomach was tied in knots. She wanted to crawl into bed and pull the covers over her head and not come out until all her problems had been magically solved.

But she also desperately wanted to see Flynn. She was becoming addicted to his smile, to the way his eyes could laugh while his face stayed completely solemn. She wasn't yet ready to put a label on all the things he made her feel, but she craved being with him.

The evening started out well enough. She'd worn the green dress as he requested. She chose it as much because she was incapable of making even the minor decision of what to wear as to please him.

Flynn's eyes warmed when he saw her, melting some of the nervous ice from around her heart. And when he kissed her, she could almost forget all the fears that had plagued her day.

He took her to another quiet restaurant. This time, they were seated in the center of the room, but there was so much space between the tables that the atmosphere remained cozy and private.

Flynn tasted the wine and nodded to the waiter before turning his full attention to Ann. "How was your day?"

"It was okay." She shrugged, feeling tension creeping into her shoulders. This felt too good, it felt too right. But she knew it wasn't right. It couldn't be right.

"It must be an incredible feeling to save someone's life."

"It is."

He leaned back as the waiter set spinach salads down in front of them. "Do you ever think about what your life might have been like if you'd become a veterinarian?"

"No!" His eyes jerked to her face and Ann flushed, realizing how abrupt the word had sounded. "I mean, why would I? I'm very fulfilled in my career. I can't imagine my life without it. Being a doctor is important work and I'm very proud of what I do."

"You should be."

Ann picked at her salad without interest. Why did the words ring so hollow? What was it about Flynn that made her feel like somebody's uptight maiden aunt? He had no right to make her feel like that. Everybody didn't have to have hobbies and take brilliant pictures that they never showed to anyone. Some people wanted to make a difference in the world. Some people had ambition.

"How was your visit to your parents?"

"Pretty much the same as always. Dad wants me to take an active role in the corporation. I don't know why he should care. He's retired now and it's running itself just fine but he feels there should be a McCallister on the board." He half laughed and, at another time, Ann might have heard the pain in the sound. "I don't know why he can't get it through his head that I'm not like Mark."

"Was Mark involved in the company? I thought he was a police officer."

"He was but he had a great head for the business. Dad always figured Mark would quit the force and join the company after a few years and he's probably right. But I don't have the least interest in the company. And I've got a lousy head for business."

"Maybe it disappoints him that you don't have more ambition."

Ann leaned back to allow the waiter to take her untouched salad plate and pretended not to notice the way Flynn's eyes widened at her tone.

"We can't all be ambitious. I'm fairly content the way I am."

"Are you? I can't believe that." Ann didn't know where the words were coming from. She just knew that she was suddenly brimming with anger and frustration that had to find an outlet.

Flynn half laughed. "Why do I have the feeling that I've done something to upset you? Is it my tie?"

"I just hate to see waste, that's all."

"One man's waste is another man's life-style," he murmured, still trying to keep the conversation light.

"You can joke all you want but you're wasting your life and you're wasting your talents."

His mouth tightened and his eyes glittered with the beginnings of temper. "It's my life to waste and they're my talents."

"You're copping out."

"Where the hell is this coming from? When I left this morning, there was a warm, responsive woman in my bed. Now, I'm sitting across the table from an uptight, driven yuppie."

The waiter approached their table with the entrées and Flynn sent him away with a flick of his hand and a look that probably seared the food on the plates.

"I'm neither uptight nor driven. I'm a reasonably ambitious woman who's chosen to make something of her life."

"Fine. Have I complained? You be ambitious and I won't be and we'll do just fine."

"It just seems to me that you're a little old to still be defying 'Daddy.' "

"I beg your pardon." The tone was icy, warning her to back off.

She gestured angrily, oblivious to the fact that the other diners were becoming aware of the altercation taking place in their midst.

"Everything you do is done to prove to your father that he can't tell you what to do. You're like a little boy, shouting defiance and hurting yourself more than anyone else. Isn't it time to grow up?"

Flynn's knuckles whitened around the delicate stem of the wineglass. His eyes glittered furiously as he looked at her. His tone was level, absolutely calm and brimming with anger.

"At least I haven't let my entire life be run by my father like you have. You've spent thirty years trying to be the perfect little girl for a man who neither notices nor cares."

"That's not true!"

"I thought you wanted the truth tonight, Dr. Perry." He continued ruthlessly. "The truth is that your father doesn't give a damn about you as a person. All he cares about is that the things you do reflect well on him.

"Sleeping with me is probably the first thing you've ever done that you didn't ask Daddy's permission for. Or did you call and check it out with him first?"

The crack of her hand against his cheek echoed in the quiet room. Flynn's head jerked slightly with the impact of the blow, but he didn't lift his hand to check the injury. His eyes seemed to burn into her.

Ann drew her hand back, pressing it against her mouth, her horrified eyes on the red imprint of her palm that was slowly darkening his lean cheek. "Oh, my God."

There was a sharp ping and she looked down to see that the stem of his wine glass had snapped in his fingers. The bowl fell to the table, spreading white wine across the table. On its heels came the darker tint of blood.

"Oh, my God."

"I believe you said that once." Flynn barely glanced at his bleeding hand. He raised his hand to the waiter, who was staring at them in stunned silence, along with the rest of the restaurant. Ann reached for his hand, responding instinctively to the sight of his injury. "Don't!" He didn't raise his voice, but something in the tone stopped her instantly.

She watched in miserable silence as he pulled a snowy handkerchief from his pocket and wrapped it around his palm, stemming the bleeding. The waiter crept up to the table, as if half-afraid that his bizarre customers might intend him some bodily harm.

"The lady and I will not be dining tonight after all. Please tell Mike to put the meal on my tab and add a healthy tip for yourself."

Flynn stood up, dropping his napkin on the table. "I think we should go now."

Ann stood up, miserably aware that every eye in the house was on them. Flynn walked behind her without touching her. She had never in her life caused a scene. Never in her life been involved in a scene. She wasn't sure which was worse, being involved in a scene or knowing that it was completely her fault.

Flynn didn't say a word as they walked out into the street. He gave the valet his ticket stub and then stood next to her, hands in pockets while they waited for the

Ferrari. Ann glanced at him once or twice. She wanted to say something but she didn't know what. He was so close but he looked a million miles away.

He saw her seated, his hand completely impersonal on her elbow. Seconds later, he was sitting beside her and the car's engine growled as he pulled away from the curb.

Ann could feel the temper that simmered in him. She half expected him to drive like a maniac, and she made up her mind to say nothing, no matter what he did. But he stayed well within the speed limit, steering the powerful car at an almost sedate pace. It was worse than if he'd speeded.

"Flynn—"

"Don't. Just forget it."

"But I—"

"Drop it." There was such command in the simple words that Ann subsided into her seat. She wasn't sure what she'd planned to say anyway. How could she apologize for the things she'd said? How could she explain all the turmoil that had built up inside her, seeking some exit and that he'd just gotten in the way.

The Ferrari came to a halt outside their building. Inside, she could see Joe sitting at his desk, his eyes registering the familiar car before going back to the book he was reading.

She glanced at Flynn but his eyes were focused out the windshield, staring at the empty street. "Aren't you coming in?"

"No. If you didn't bring your key, Joe can let you in."

"I have my key. Flynn—"

"Goodbye, Ann."

He didn't look at her. It was as if, in his mind, she'd already ceased to exist. Ann blinked back unwanted tears and reached for the latch, stepping out onto the sidewalk. Flynn leaned across the seat and pulled the door shut, putting the car into gear immediately.

Ann watched the sleek black sports car disappear around a corner, the well-bred howl of the engine sounding loud in the quiet night. The air was still warm but she shivered. She felt as if she'd just lost something incredibly important. She stood there a long time, half hoping that he'd return, that he'd give her a chance to explain the inexplicable.

But he didn't come back.

Ann let herself in, gave Joe a strained smile and went upstairs to her quiet apartment. Oscar greeted her with a meow of inquiry, clearly pleased to see her, but the cat's pleasure couldn't begin to fill the aching hollow that was opening up in her chest.

For the first time since she was a child, Ann cried herself to sleep.

THE NEXT FEW DAYS were an exercise in torture. Ann could not stop going over the disastrous evening in her mind. The events replayed themselves like a broken record: each word, each gesture, had to be taken out and examined again and again.

She'd deliberately set out to pick a fight with Flynn. There was no other possible explanation. She'd been looking for a reason to break off their relationship, looking for some terrible flaw in him. She'd found a flaw, but it was in herself, not in Flynn.

One thing she'd always prided herself on was her ability to face reality. She tried never to lie to herself. Yet, she'd buried her head in the sand when it came to

Flynn McCallister. From the moment she'd moved in, she'd used hostility to camouflage a powerful sexual attraction. Even then, she'd sensed that he could be a threat to her neatly ordered world, and she'd done everything she could to keep him at arm's length.

Then Becky had dropped into their lives and she'd been forced to look at the real Flynn, not the mythical, womanizing creation of her imagination, but the real man. The man who took in a little girl who had no one else and gave her a home. The man who captured such sensitive images on film. The man who'd taught her about passion.

The man she'd fallen in love with.

Ann leaned her head back against the wall of the elevator and closed her eyes. It was not exactly the most romantic of locations to realize that she'd fallen in love. No—she couldn't really say that she was just now realizing it. She was just now admitting it to herself, but some part of her had known it for a long time. That's why she'd been so frightened. That was why she'd struck out at him, pushing him away because she was afraid to let him get any closer.

The elevator came to a halt and the doors slid open. Ann stepped out, her head bent over her purse as she searched for her keys.

"Excuse me." Her head jerked up, her heart pounding. Flynn was standing not two feet away. It had only been three days since she'd seen him, but Ann drank in the sight of him as if it had been months.

He was wearing tailored slacks and a blue shirt that echoed the brilliance of his eyes. His hair was combed into neat black waves and Ann couldn't imagine anyone had ever looked more handsome.

"Excuse me." He repeated the polite phrase and she realized she was blocking the elevator. A hundred words surged to her lips but she didn't speak any of them. This came too close on the heels of her realization of her love for him. She felt too raw, too vulnerable.

She stepped out of the way without a word. Flynn nodded, his eyes as cool and distant as the Sierras. His shoulder almost touched hers as he stepped into the elevator. Ann didn't move until she heard the doors slide quietly shut behind her.

She saw him twice more in the next three days. Each time she ached with the need to say something—anything—to break through the terrible wall that lay between them. But she said nothing, did nothing. Just looking at him seemed to paralyze her vocal cords.

A week after the disastrous dinner date, her father came to see her. They'd spoken very little since he'd called the Social Services department to report Becky. Typically, he'd never apologized, apparently not seeing the need to do so.

Ann was seeing him in a new light. Flynn's words might have hurt but they had sunk in. She didn't want to believe that he was right. Of course her father cared about her.

"I understand that little girl McCallister was keeping is gone now." Robert Perry leaned back in his chair and sipped at the coffee his daughter had just handed him. Not the instant she usually made for herself but freshly ground, freshly brewed coffee. He didn't believe in instant.

"Becky is with her father now."

"Good. Best for all concerned. Gets McCallister out of your life, lets you concentrate on your career."

Ann sipped her coffee, trying not to be irritated by the cavalier way he dismissed Becky. She looked at Oscar who was lying on the back of the sofa directly across from her father. Oscar was staring at him, his golden eyes unblinking.

Robert Perry looked at him and then looked away and then looked at him again. Ann took another sip of coffee, hiding her smile in her cup. Her father shifted uneasily beneath the cat's steady regard.

"Does he always stare like that?"

"Not always." She could have gotten up and shut Oscar in her bedroom but she didn't move.

"Animals. Never could understand why anyone would want to have one."

"Oscar keeps me company." She kept her tone mild.

"Animals belong in a barnyard, not in a house. Keep them where they belong and everybody would be happier."

"I'm afraid Oscar is spoiled. I don't think he'd like a barnyard at all."

Oscar continued to stare and her father shifted again, apparently looking for a position that would shield him from the cat's impassive gaze.

"Animals. Don't know why you like them. Nasty, dirty things."

"Actually, Oscar is extremely clean." Ann set her cup down with careful deliberation. "I've been thinking about giving up my practice and going back to school."

"School! What on earth for? You've had all the training you need."

"Not to be a veterinarian." The words could not have had stronger results if she'd just announced that she was going to become a terrorist.

"Veterinarian!" He made the word sound like an obscenity. "Don't be ridiculous!"

"Dad, I'm not happy with my work. It's not that it isn't worthwhile. It just isn't what I want to do. I love animals and I love medicine. I'd like to combine the two." Her tone pleaded with him to understand. She might as well have been talking to the coffeepot.

"I forbid it! I don't know where you got this asinine idea but I absolutely forbid it."

"Dad, I'm not happy where I am. I want to try something else. There's nothing wrong with that."

"There's everything in the world wrong with it. A veterinarian. Hah! Do you think I spent all that money for your schooling just to watch you throw it all away on a whim?"

"This isn't a whim. I've given this a lot of thought and I think this will make me happy. Don't you want me to be happy?" There was a little-girl-lost quality in the question, but it was lost on him.

"Happy? What's happy got to do with it? People these days think that's all life is about. Well, it isn't. Life is about getting somewhere, accomplishing things, making something of yourself.

"I see where you get this stupid notion. It's that McCallister boy, isn't it? He's filled your head with a lot of twaddle. The man's a bum. He may not be in the street but that's only because his family has money. What's he accomplished in his life? Nothing, that's what. And he never will accomplish anything because he's a bum. Look at him. Is that the kind of life you want to live? Nobody respects him, nobody knows his name.''

"*I* respect him."

"Just shows how far he's turned your head. I should never have let you move in here. Should have stopped it the minute I found out he was living across the hall. You'll move out immediately. You can move home and we'll get these stupid notions out of your head."

Ann stared at him, not wanting to believe what she was seeing. "Dad, can't you hear what I'm saying? This has nothing to do with Flynn, though he's the one who made me see how foolish it is to waste my life. *I'm not happy.* I want to do something else with my life. Don't you want to see me happy?"

"I want to be proud of you. I want people to know that my daughter is a success. I can't be proud of someone who's wasting their time on a bunch of filthy animals."

He glared at her, and Ann looked at him over an abyss so vast that there was no crossing it. Later it would hurt, but right now she felt numbed by the weight of all the years she wasted trying to please him.

"You don't care about me at all, do you? Not about me as a person."

"Don't be melodramatic. Of course I care. You're my daughter."

"But I'm not a person to you at all, am I? I'm just an extension of yourself. Something that you can point at for people to admire."

He stood up. "I think it would be best if I left before you say something you'll regret. I've always had your best interests at heart, Ann. When you've calmed down, you'll see that I'm right about this, too."

"I don't think so."

She listened to the door close behind him and waited for all the pain to come crashing down on her. But the only feeling that emerged was a tremendous relief. As if she'd known all along, and getting it out in the open had lifted the burden from her.

Ann didn't know how long she sat there thinking. All the turmoil of the past few weeks was suddenly gone and her mind was working clearly. She knew exactly what she wanted out of life. It was so clear that she couldn't understand how she could have let herself get so muddled about it.

And the first step was to find Flynn. Nothing else in her life could be right until he was back in it. Flynn was the key to everything. Why hadn't she seen that from the start?

She stood up so abruptly that it startled Oscar, almost making him lose his balance. He dug his claws into the linen of the sofa to keep from falling and gave her an indignant look as she hurried by. But Ann didn't notice. She had more important things on her mind.

She knocked on Flynn's door and waited impatiently for him to answer. She wasn't exactly sure what she wanted to say but she knew the words would come once she saw him. He would understand. He had to understand.

She knocked again, waiting for a long time before finally admitting that he wasn't home. She leaned her forehead against his door as if she could will him to be there.

"I've got it all straightened out now, Flynn. Where are you?" The whisper went unanswered.

Chapter Thirteen

"That was terrific, Mom." Flynn pushed his plate away and dropped his napkin beside it.

"You hardly ate enough to keep a bird alive. Are you sure you got enough?"

"I think that theory has been proven false. Didn't I read somewhere that birds have to eat twice their weight every day? If I ate enough to keep a bird alive, you'd have to roast another chicken or three."

His mother smiled but he read the worry in her eyes. He looked away. He knew that she could sense that something was wrong but he wasn't ready to talk about it. Not yet. The hurt was too new, too raw.

He reached for his wine, sipping it slowly. The crisp chardonnay was a far cry from the things he'd been drinking this last week. Stupid. It shamed him to think of how much time he'd spent drinking since the fight with Ann. There were no answers to be found at the bottom of a bottle. He knew that, and he hadn't really been looking for answers. He'd been looking for oblivion. Only that wasn't to be found, either.

It didn't matter how drunk he got, he could still remember his losses. Mark, who'd died much too young, leaving so many unanswered questions and

leaving Flynn with a burden of perfection he felt woefully inadequate to carry. Becky, darting in and out of
his life and changing it completely. And Ann. God,
how could he describe that loss? She'd given him a
glimpse of heaven and then snatched it back.

Maybe she was right. Maybe the fault was his. He
should have more ambition. Maybe if he'd tried
harder to please his father, Mark wouldn't have had to
carry the whole burden. Maybe he wouldn't have died.

Flynn shook his head. Stupid. He was what he was
just as Mark had chosen his path. He couldn't make
himself something he wasn't, just as his brother hadn't
been able to be something he wasn't.

"Flynn!" Flynn's head jerked up at his father's
sharp command and he realized that he'd been staring at the tablecloth, completely absorbed in his
thoughts. David McCallister frowned at him sternly
from across the table. "Your mother is speaking to
you."

"I'm sorry, Mom. What were you saying?"

"Your mother shouldn't have to repeat herself.
Have you been drinking? You act like you're only half
awake." His father jabbed irritably at a steamed car-
rot and Flynn wondered if he was wishing it was his
son he was poking.

"I haven't had anything today but I could change
that if you'd like." The smile he gave his father was
designed to make the older man's blood pressure rise.
Their eyes fenced in an old challenge, one that neither of them had ever won.

"Flynn. David. Stop it, both of you." The look
Louise gave her husband and son could have controlled an entire army. It served quite well with her
family.

"Sorry, Mom."

David muttered into his coffee cup. The words might have been an apology or they might have been a curse. His wife chose not to ask for clarification.

The rest of the meal passed without incident. No one was in the mood for the chocolate pie the cook had made and left for the meal. The three of them adjourned to the study and, with a worried look at her husband and son, Louise left to make coffee.

When she returned, they were exactly where she'd left them. Her husband was seated in his favorite chair, his gaze focused on the wall opposite. Flynn leaned one shoulder against the mantel, his eyes on the snifter of brandy he held. It was raining outside, the first big storm of the season and a small fire crackled in the fireplace, more for psychological warmth than to supplement the heating. But it didn't seem to have done much good. The atmosphere in the room was chill with old hurts.

Louise sighed faintly as she wheeled the coffee tray into the room. She settled herself in a chair across from her husband, near the warmth from the fireplace. David accepted a cup of coffee from her but Flynn lifted the brandy snifter in silent refusal. She caught David's eye on his son and hurried into speech before he could comment on Flynn's drinking.

"Have you heard from Becky?"

"I got a letter yesterday." His face softened in the first real smile she'd seen since his arrival. "The spelling was a little shaky but I gather that she's happy. Rafferty took her into the mountains to see the snow and she's pretty impressed with it. They had a snowball fight and she won. The house is great and there's a huge backyard with a big tree. Rafferty has promised her a swing this summer.''

"It sounds like she's happy. I'm so glad. She's a sweet child.''

"Yes, she is. I miss her but it helps to know that she's happy. I know Rafferty is going to be a great father.''

"It could have been such a tragedy. I think it's wonderful that everything worked out so well. How is Ann? She must be missing Becky, too.''

Flynn's smile faded and his eyes dropped back to his drink. "I'm sure she is. Ann and I aren't seeing each other these days.''

He said it casually, but his mother could hear the pain underlying the words and her heart went out to him. Mark had always been the serious one, but Louise knew which of her sons felt pain most deeply. Flynn had always been so good at hiding his feelings, but his emotions ran deep.

"I'm sorry, Flynn.''

He shrugged, his smile twisted. "So am I, Mom.''

"Figures. Thought the girl had too much sense to be seeing you.''

"David!'' Louise's shocked exclamation brought a flush to her husband's face.

"No, that's all right, Mom. It's not like Dad's opinion of me is anything new, is it, Dad? Families should be honest with one another.''

David's flush deepened at the sweet sarcasm in Flynn's tone. "The trouble with you, Flynn, is that you've got a chip on your shoulder. You're always looking to blame someone else for your troubles.''

"I don't blame anyone for anything, Dad.''

"And you lack sense. Any half-wit could see that Ann was a woman worth keeping. What do you do? You let her go."

"What do you suggest I should have done? Chained her in the basement?" Flynn's smile stayed in place but his knuckles whitened on the brandy snifter. "She seemed to think that one of my major flaws was that I was too much like my father. Amusing, don't you think?"

David McCallister didn't see the humor. "Like me? Ha! Thought the girl had more sense. I can't imagine two people less alike."

"For once, we agree on something." Flynn lifted his glass in a mock toast.

"The trouble with you, Flynn, is that you lack any real direction. A man needs a career, something to focus his energies on."

"Dad, I focus my energies on enjoying life. That's enough of a career for me."

"Stop it, both of you." Louise's voice interrupted the budding argument. "I don't want to listen to this. Honestly. I don't understand why the two of you can't get along."

"Bad blood, Mom." Flynn shook his head mournfully. "I've inherited bad blood from your side of the family. No McCallister could ever be so worthless. You'll just have to live with the fact that you've tainted the McCallister line."

"Hah! What McCallister line?" Flynn winced at his father's barked comment. "There is no McCallister line anymore and there's not likely to be. Now, when your brother was alive, there was some hope for it. *He* had some sense."

"David."

He stood up; his frustration was too great to let him stay still. His eyes were on his younger son, anger and confusion in their depths.

"Don't 'David' me, Louise. It's not as if I'm saying something that we don't all know already. Mark would never have wasted his life the way his brother is doing. Mark had ambition. He had pride—in himself and in the family name."

"Mark didn't give a holy damn about the family name. Mark wanted to please you and he spent his whole life trying to do it." Flynn stopped with an effort, setting his jaw against the urge to say more.

"And what's wrong with wanting to please your father? Seems to me to be a worthwhile thing to do."

"There's nothing wrong with it. Look, Dad, why don't you just give up? I'm never going to be the model son Mark was."

"Don't think I don't know that." The older man's tone was bitter and Flynn whitened at the bite in the words. He set the brandy snifter down on the mantel. The faint ping of the crystal hitting the marble sounded too loud.

"Mark was a son a man could be proud of. If he hadn't been killed in the line of duty, he'd probably have presented me with a grandson by now. Instead, I'm left with you. A playboy." His tone made the word a curse. "A man who hasn't amounted to anything and never will."

Flynn felt something snap inside. It was as if he were suddenly standing outside himself, watching this confrontation. "I don't think that's too likely." The words seemed to come from somewhere outside himself.

"You don't think what's too likely? That you'll amount to anything? I know it's not likely."

"I don't think it's too likely that Mark would have presented you with a grandson by now."

"Flynn, no!" He heard his mother's hushed protest, but it didn't penetrate the wall of pain that seemed to be tearing him apart.

"Mark was gay." Father and son stared at each other across a gap that had been there for more years than either could remember. As soon as the words were said, Flynn wanted to call them back. He'd never planned to say them. Never wanted to hurt his father with them.

The older man stared into his son's horrified eyes, reading the truth there. He seemed to shrink and age in a matter of minutes. He groped behind him for his chair, his movements shaken.

Flynn took a quick step forward, his hand coming out, but his father waved him away with a look of loathing so intense it seemed to burn into his soul. He sank into the chair, his hands gripping the arms, his knuckles white.

The stillness was thick, almost a presence in itself. Outside the rain poured down, splashing onto the brick terrace. Inside the fire popped, sending sparks shooting up the chimney. The sound, like the sparks, was swallowed instantly.

"You're lying." David McCallister's voice sounded old and feeble. There was no trace of his usual blustering tones. Flynn didn't hesitate. He'd have done anything to take the shattered look out of his father's eyes.

"You're right. It was a lie. I'm sorry." He backed away, picking up his brandy, his hand clenched over the crystal snifter.

"You're sorry? You're sorry?"

"David, please..." Louise might as well have remained silent.

"You impudent bastard!"

Flynn shrugged, staring at the glass he held. "I'm sorry, Dad. I shouldn't have said it."

"You were jealous of him. You were always jealous of him." David's voice rose with each sentence. "He was everything a man could have wanted in a son. I couldn't have expected to have two sons like him but I can't believe I fathered a sniveling bastard like you."

"Don't feel too bad. It happens in the best of families." Flynn's flippant remark cracked at the end, but his father was too enraged to notice.

"Get out. Get out of this house. I don't ever want to see you again." Flynn whitened, his eyes burning in his face as he stared at his father. "Do you hear me? Get out!"

Flynn lifted the snifter and tossed the last of the fine cognac down his throat, feeling it burn all the way down. His smile was twisted, his eyes empty.

"To happy families." He set the snifter down on the mantel and strode from the room.

Louise looked from her husband's shattered face to her son's rigid back. In the space of a minute, her family had been torn apart. If it was ever to be put back together again, it would be up to her. She rose from her chair and hurried after Flynn. He was tugging his leather jacket off the coat rack when she caught him.

"Flynn."

He turned and tears filled her eyes at the shattered look in his eyes. He shrugged into his jacket.

"You should be with him. He's pretty upset."

"I'll go to him in a minute. I wanted to talk to you."

"Don't worry, Mom, I'm not going to wrap my car around a telephone pole."

She caught his hands in hers. "Flynn, give him some time. He didn't really mean it. He'll come around."

He pulled his hands loose and touched her cheek, his fingers gentle. His smile broke her heart; there was so much loss there.

"Some wounds not even time can heal. Don't worry about me. I'll be all right."

He was gone before she could say anything more. There was a moment when the door was open to the rain-swept night and then it shut, closing her inside and shutting him out. She stared at the blank panel a long time, hearing the growl of the Ferrari's engine disappearing down the drive.

She turned slowly, walking back into the study. Her husband was slumped in his chair, his features old and worn. She hardened her heart against his suffering. Flynn was suffering, too. And had suffered for a long time.

"It's not true. How could he say something like that about his own brother?" The words were muttered, his eyes shifting away from hers.

Louise knew what David wanted. He wanted her to say that he was right, that Flynn had lied. He wanted her to right his world for him. But she couldn't do that.

She sat down, reaching out to take his hands in hers, stilling their restless movements. "David, the only thing that's important is that Mark was a wonderful son. He was good and kind and we were very lucky to have him with us for as long as we did."

"I know that! I just don't know how we could have ended up with a son like Flynn. He's a changeling, that's what he is."

"No, David. Flynn is as much your son as Mark was. More perhaps." Her fingers tightened over his, stilling his indignant protest. "You and Flynn are too much alike. Neither of you knows how to give an inch. Mark was willing to bend. He let you shape him. But Flynn knew just who he was from the time he was a baby and he never let you bully him into anything."

"I never bullied Mark!"

"You didn't have to. Mark was content to do what you wanted. But Flynn wanted to go his own way. Just like his father always did."

She paused, letting that sink in, seeing the way his eyes shifted away from hers, as if trying to avoid the truth in her words.

"He's pigheaded and shiftless."

"He's no more pigheaded than you are. And he's doing exactly what he wants to do. How can that be shiftless?"

"He doesn't show proper respect."

"Have you ever shown him any respect?"

He glared at her for a moment and then looked away, staring into the fireplace. "I never knew what to do with him. He'd look at me with those bright blue eyes, listen to what I said and then do exactly what he wanted."

"Are you any different?"

He grunted, unwilling to agree, unable to argue.

"David, we've already lost one son. Mark is gone and we can't ever get him back. I don't want to lose my

other son and I don't think you do, either. Flynn has
tried all his life to be friends with you. Don't you think
it's time that you tried just a little? If you don't reach
out, we're going to lose him. *You're* going to lose him.
Just as surely as we did Mark.''

He didn't say anything, only continued to stare into
the flames. With a sigh, she squeezed his hands and
moved away. She'd tried all she could. She could only
pray that she'd gotten through to him. Time would
tell.

Chapter Fourteen

The rain poured down with a steady persistence that said it was here to stay for a long time. Ann stared out the sliding glass door on to the neatly tended rooftop garden and wondered if it was possible to feel any more depressed than she did at that moment.

It was after one o'clock in the morning. She'd been knocking on Flynn's door every half an hour since eight. At one point, she'd even gone down to the garage to make sure he wasn't home and just refusing to answer the door. But the Ferrari was gone and so was Flynn.

Where was he? She tried not to think of what she would do if he arrived home with a woman on his arm. She couldn't bear to lose him now. Not when she'd finally realized that he was what she needed. How could she have been so blind? Why hadn't she seen weeks ago that she was in love with him?

She stepped away from the window and drew the curtains shut, closing out the stormy night. What if he'd had an accident? With the storm soaking the streets, the roads would be dangerous. She could stand anything, just as long as he was safe.

She sat down on the sofa, staring into the fireplace. She'd built a fire earlier but it was down to embers now, a sullen red glow that seemed more dark than light. Oscar was asleep on a chair, there was not a sound in the apartment except for the occasional crackle of the dying fire and the steady drone of the rain.

Ann leaned her head back, closing her eyes. She had to talk to Flynn. It couldn't be too late for them. It just couldn't.

She had no idea how much later it was that she was startled upright. She hadn't been aware of falling asleep until she was shocked awake. Oscar was crouched on the back of the sofa, his fur on end, obviously disturbed by whatever it was that had awakened his mistress. The knock on the door came again, sounding loud in the quiet night.

Ann stumbled to her feet, groggy and disoriented. She tugged at her loose shirt and pushed her hair out of her face before reaching for the doorknob, her mind still blank with sleep. She pulled the door open and all her thoughts shifted into instant focus.

Flynn stood outside. A Flynn she'd never seen before. He was soaking wet, from the black hair that molded his head to the snakeskin boots that glistened with water. Water dripped off of him, creating little puddles before soaking into the thick carpeting. All of this, she noticed peripherally. What caught her and held her was his eyes.

Their brilliant blue was dulled to steely gray. His skin looked pale and his face seemed much older than his years. He looked like a man who'd seen the death of all his dreams and had nothing left inside. He looked absolutely shattered.

She stared at him in stunned silence, her shocked eyes taking in his condition. His mouth quirked in a frail ghost of a smile and his eyes dropped from hers to stare at the damp floor.

"I know it's late. I...didn't know where else to go." His voice was hollow, lost. Ann felt as if her heart were breaking. Whatever he'd been through, it had drained him of all the vibrancy she'd come to associate with him.

She reached out, taking his hand, feeling the chill of his skin. "Come in." He stumbled as he stepped in, catching himself against the wall.

"Sorry."

"You're frozen. Come in by the fire. I'll throw a couple more logs on and get it stoked up."

He let her strip the ruined leather jacket off his shoulders. "I didn't know where else to go." He repeated the words as if it were the only coherent thought in his mind.

His shirt was as wet as the rest of him. "What happened?"

He stared at her blankly and she expanded on the question. "Why are you so wet?"

"The Ferrari ran out of gas. I've been walking."

"How long did you walk?"

"I don't know. I just walked."

"Well, you're soaked to the skin. I want you to go get in a hot shower. I'll go to your place and get you something to put on."

He seemed to come out of his fog somewhat. He ran his fingers through his hair, only just then realizing how wet he was. "I'm sorry. I'm probably ruining your carpet. I should go home."

"Don't be ridiculous. Go take a shower. I'll go get some dry clothes and make some coffee." She gave him a push in the direction of the bathroom, waiting until she heard the shower start before getting the key he'd given her when Becky was staying with him and letting herself into his apartment.

By the time Flynn got out of the shower, Ann had made coffee and sandwiches and thrown enough logs on the fire to create a roaring blaze. Flynn looked a little less like the walking dead when he stepped out of the bathroom. She'd brought him fresh jeans and a heavy flannel shirt and, if it hadn't been for the dampness of his hair, it might have been possible to imagine that the two of them had been sitting in front of a fire all night.

"I didn't know if you'd be hungry."

He sank onto the sofa and glanced at the coffee and sandwiches. "The coffee looks great but I'm really not hungry. It was nice of you to fix them, though."

She handed him a cup of steaming coffee, her eyes going over him carefully. He looked better. There was still that rather frightening emptiness at the back of his eyes but his skin was not quite so gaunt.

The silence grew between them. Oddly enough, it wasn't an uncomfortable silence. The rain continued to pound down on the roof tops outside, filling the void with its hypnotic rhythm.

"What happened?"

Flynn had been staring into the flames and it was a moment before he dragged his gaze to her, his eyes reflecting the fire. He was quiet so long, his eyes looking almost through her, that Ann began to wonder if he'd even heard her question.

"I went to visit my parents. My father and I had a fight."

Ann waited, but he didn't seem to have anything else to say. "I thought you and your father quarreled pretty often."

"We do." He stirred abruptly, his eyes dropping to the mug he held. "This time was...different. This time I don't think we're going to be able to forget it."

Ann hesitated, wondering if she had the right to probe, her instincts telling her that he needed to talk about whatever it was that was eating into him.

"I know I may not seem like the best candidate but I've been known to lend a sympathetic ear."

Flynn glanced up, smiling briefly. "I know."

Silence settled between them again. Ann waited, knowing that the next move had to come from him. He finished his coffee and reached forward to pour a fresh cup, settling back against the cushions and staring into the fire, his expression brooding.

"I suppose we quarreled about you indirectly." He spoke so abruptly that Ann jumped.

"Me? What about me?"

"He thinks you were smart to get rid of me. He agrees with your opinions. He thinks I'm a worthless, ambitionless playboy."

"Flynn, I didn't mean those things I said." Her fingers knotted around her cup, her heart breaking at the thought that she could be the cause of his misery.

He glanced at her again, his smile sweet. "You know what's funny? It hurt when you said it but I knew you didn't mean it. Not like he meant it. You were right about a lot of what you said. I do still do some things just to prove that my father's opinion of me is right. And I suppose I don't have a whole hell of a lot of ambition but then, I've never seen ambition as being the be-all-and-end-all of life.''

"Flynn, what did your father say to you?'' She had to know what had put that look in his eyes.

"It wasn't what he said to me. It's what I said to him." His mouth twisted bitterly, his eyes on the fire. "I broke a promise. I broke a promise and I did it because I was hurt and I wanted to lash out and hurt back. Not a very good reason.''

"What promise, Flynn?''

"My father was riding me about my life, my personality, my future. All the usual stuff. I should be used to it by now." He set the cup down and stood up, moving to crouch by the fire and pick up the poker. He jabbed at the logs, sending flames shooting up the chimney.

"And then he started telling me how, if Mark had lived, Mark would have given him a grandson by now." He stood up, leaning his forearm against the mantel and staring down into the flames. "I told him that wasn't likely. It's the truth but, God help me, I had no right to say it.''

Ann stared at his taut figure, a vague suspicion forming in the back of her mind. "Why wouldn't Mark have given him a grandson?''

He turned his head to look at her and she almost cried out at the self-loathing in his eyes. "Mark was gay. Mr. Captain-of-the-football-team, tough-cop. God, how he hated himself. He hated himself for being what he was. He said Dad would never be able to stand the shock if he found out and I kept his secret for him. I kept it all these years until tonight. Tonight, I blurted it out like a child. Just because I was hurt. My father called me a bastard. I can't even blame him.'' He put his head down, resting his forehead on his arm, his shoulders slumped in absolute defeat.

Ann got up and went to him. All the hurt that lay between them was forgotten. This was the man she loved and he was in pain. All she wanted was to ease his hurts. He resisted her arms when they slid around his waist but Ann ignored him, pressing her forehead against his taut back, holding him.

"Flynn, you're only human. I'm sure Mark would understand what you did. And your father will come around. Just give him some time. He was hurt and shocked but he'll come around."

He held himself away from her a moment longer and she thought she'd lost, that he wasn't going to take the comfort she offered, that he wasn't going to be able to let down the barriers he'd built up over the years.

He turned suddenly, almost throwing her off balance, his arms going around her and clutching her convulsively tight. Ann lifted herself on her toes, circling his neck with her arms as he buried his face in her loose hair.

They stood that way for a long time. Ann stroked his hair, wanting to soothe away years of hurt. Beside them the fire snapped and popped. Outside, the rain poured down on the city, washing clean the summer's accumulation of dirt.

Inside, there was just the two of them. No past, no future, nothing but the present. Ann felt the dampness of his tears on her neck and her arms tightened. She wanted to tell him that everything was going to be all right, but she couldn't get the words out past the lump in her throat. She could only hold him, offering the only comfort she could.

Inside, a part of her was singing with elation. He'd come to her. In his misery, he'd come to her. That had to mean that he cared. He wouldn't have come to her if he didn't care for her.

She didn't know how long it was before he moved, his arms loosening around her. He backed away, wiping self-consciously at the dampness on his cheeks. His eyes looked anywhere but at her.

"It's late. I shouldn't have kept you up so late."

"It's all right."

He glanced at her and then looked away. "I should go home."

It was Ann's turn to look away. "You could stay here tonight."

The silence seemed to stretch out endlessly. Neither of them looked at the other, but it was in both their minds that they'd reached a major turning point.

"I'd like that." Ann let out her breath in a rush, only then aware that she'd been holding it.

They didn't turn on lights in the bedroom. They undressed in the dark, without speaking. They weren't ready for words. Ann slipped on a silk sleepshirt and slid onto the cool cotton sheets. A moment later, Flynn joined her.

They lay apart for a few moments, each uncertain of the other's expectations. So much had been said but there was so much left to say. Flynn's hand slid across the inches that separated them, seeking her arm. It was all the invitation Ann needed. With her head nestled securely against his shoulder, the strong beat of his heart beneath her palm, she felt as if she'd come home.

Within minutes, he was asleep, his breath stirring her hair. But, even in sleep, his arms held her securely. Despite the late hour, Ann lay awake, staring into the darkness. He needed her. The realization slipped into her mind with the softness of a whisper, but the impact was much greater. With that realization came another. All these weeks, she'd been so afraid of falling in love with him, terrified of being vulnerable. She finally knew why.

Flynn seemed so complete in himself. He'd never seemed to need anyone. In his own flip way, he'd always been invulnerable. It was frightening to need someone so much and feel that the need was one-sided.

But, tonight, she'd seen the vulnerability in him. She'd seen what she had to offer him. An unconditional love. Someone who accepted him with all his faults and all his good points. Someone who'd never compare him to another and find him wanting.

Someone who'd love him just as he was.

WHEN FLYNN WOKE, he was alone. He rolled over in bed, his arm sweeping out in search of Ann's warmth, but the bed was empty and the sheets were cool. He opened his eyes, feeling strangely empty. He stared at the ceiling, exploring his emotions, seeking the source of the emptiness.

Mark. For the first time in three years, he was not carrying the hard knot of pain that had been there since his brother's death. He called his brother's face to mind and was surprised to find that it had grown slightly fuzzy around the edges. The warmth in the eyes, the smile, those were still crisp and clear, but other details were blurred. Softened.

Softened. That was how the pain felt. It was still there. He'd never stop missing Mark. The loss would always be with him. But the pain had softened, become bearable. It was as if, in talking about him, really talking about him, the memories had fallen into their proper place.

He sat up, his eyes skimming over the room. It was the first time he'd been in Ann's bedroom, and he found it looked just as he'd expected it to look. Neat and tidy, almost like a motel room except for the occasional touches that showed the woman lying beneath the career.

Her closet was partially open, and he grinned when he saw the tangle of shoes that covered the bottom. He would have expected her to have her shoes neatly lined up on shelves, carefully paired and labeled with the days of the week. There was an extravagantly feminine vanity in one corner, its surface covered with delicate perfume bottles. Funny, he'd never associated Ann with perfume.

His curiosity aroused, he slid out of bed and walked over to the vanity to pick up an exquisite crystal flagon. It was empty, as were all the other bottles, and his grin deepened. She collected perfume bottles. He remembered their discussion about hobbies and wondered why she hadn't told him about this. Funny, how she seemed almost ashamed of the frivolous side of her.

He set the bottle down and walked into the bathroom, picking up his clothing on the way. He took a long shower, wondering what he was going to say to Ann when he saw her. He'd never opened himself up to another person like he had to her. Not even to Mark. He wondered what she'd say. She loved him.

He was sure of it. Or maybe he was only sure of it because it was what he desperately wanted to believe.

She had to love him. If she didn't, he didn't know what he was going to do.

Ann was making coffee when she heard the bedroom door open. She spilled grounds onto the counter and quickly scooped them up, trying to control the shaking of her hands. What was he going to say? How was he going to act? Was he going to pretend that last night had never happened?

She turned, hoping her smile looked more confident than it felt. He was standing in the kitchen doorway and she couldn't imagine how it was possible for a man to look so gorgeous. He was wearing the same jeans and flannel shirt she'd brought over for him the night before. He'd rolled the sleeves up on the shirt and his feet were bare. His hair looked like he'd combed it with his fingers and his jaw was shadowed with beard. He'd never looked better.

"Good morning." His voice was husky but whether from sleep or nerves, Ann couldn't guess. "Looks like the storm's over."

She nodded, glancing over her shoulder at the sunshine that spilled in through the window over the sink. "Looks like a beautiful day."

She tugged at the hem of her loose cotton sweater, wishing she'd taken time to put on more makeup, wishing she was wearing something more flattering. Wishing he'd say something to break the tension.

"I love you."

The words dropped into the tense silence like a boulder into a pond. There was the initial splash and then ripples rushed outward, throwing Ann off balance. Her head jerked up, her eyes meeting his. He was still leaning in the door in the same casual position, but now she could see the tension in his shoulders, the tautness of his body.

"Oh God." She slumped back against the counter, her knees shaking.

His brows shot up. "Oh God? Is that horror or pleased surprise?" The question was flip but she knew him too well now. She could see how much her answer meant to him.

"I've been trying to figure out how to apologize for the awful things I said to you at that horrible dinner. I've been agonizing how to go about carefully building a relationship. I've been..." He was across the kitchen in an instant, his arms going around her, holding her close.

"You've been talking too much. Do you love me or do I go jump off the balcony?"

She rested her head on his chest, feeling the way his heart pounded beneath her cheek. Her mouth turned up in a smile. Never again would she fall for his flippant, I-don't-give-a-damn act.

"I love you." His arms tightened, drawing a squeak of protest from her.

"I still don't have any ambition."

"I know. I've always wanted to live with a bum."

"I will probably never have any ambition."

"That's okay. I've got enough for both of us."

"I—"

"Will you just shut up and kiss me, for crying out loud."

His hand slid into her hair, tilting her head back until he could look into her eyes. The look of love he read there wiped away the last traces of pain. Years of loneliness melted in her love.

"What did I ever do to deserve you?"

She smiled at him, her eyes sparkling through a film of tears. "I don't know. It must have been something pretty terrific."

"It must have been."

His mouth came down on hers, smothering any reply she might have made.

Oscar trotted into the kitchen and studied the two humans for a moment. It was time for breakfast, but the cat could see that they weren't going to be thinking of anything practical for a long time to come. Being a tactful feline, he turned and left the room.

Epilogue

"What do you think you're doing?"

Ann jumped at the barked question, jerking her head out of the box she'd been packing and spinning around to face her husband.

Flynn looked at her sternly, a look not in the least softened by the fact that his hair stood on end and his face was streaked with dirt.

"I'm packing a box. What did it look like I was doing?"

"You're not supposed to be doing things like that."

"Things like what? Flynn, I was packing some china, not a cast-iron stove."

"I don't care. You're supposed to be sitting back and watching me work." He picked his way through the turmoil of packing boxes until he reached her side. Taking her by the arm, he led her to the sofa, shoving stacks of linen onto the floor to make room for her.

"Flynn, I'm two months pregnant. I'm not sick. I'm not injured. Pregnancy is a perfectly normal function of the human body and there's no reason to treat me like an invalid."

He crouched in front of her, reaching up to tuck a stray lock of hair beneath the scarf she was wearing.

"Indulge me. I've only been a father to be for a week. I'm still in the crazy stage."

She reached out to smooth his hair, feeling her love well up inside. "You're always in the crazy stage. You're going to make a great father."

"I like to think so. Ouch!" He gave her a hurt look, reaching up to remove her fingers from the strand of hair she'd just tugged. "What was that for?"

"To keep you from getting overconfident."

"I think I've got something to be overconfident about. After all, we decide we want a baby and you get pregnant the first month of trying. I think that says something about my manly prowess."

He looked so smug that Ann couldn't help but laugh. "It says more about your appetites. Considering how many times you ravished me, it would have been more amazing if I *hadn't* gotten pregnant."

"I don't remember you kicking and screaming."

She smiled, running her fingers over a streak of dirt on his cheek. "No. I suppose I wasn't. Are you really, truly happy about this baby?"

"Ann, I am really, truly happy about everything. You. The baby. Moving. My life couldn't be more perfect."

Her eyes grew dreamy. "We'll have to start thinking of names. If it's a girl, we could name her Rebecca, after Becky."

He shook his head. "No. There's only one Becky. Besides, since we're going to be moving into her neighborhood, it would get confusing with two little girls named Becky."

"I suppose. Rafferty called last night. He says he's got all the real estate ads marked for us. Becky's looking forward to helping us pick out a house."

"Just as long as she doesn't cook dinner for us. Are you sure this is what you want to do? We're making a lot of changes all at once. You quitting your job, moving to a new state, trying to get into school and having a baby. It's a lot to take on."

"I'm not pushing any of it." She smiled at him, feeling contentment fill her. A year of marriage hadn't softened the intensity of their love. Flynn had become her champion, her companion, her lover. She'd never thought it possible to be so happy. He'd supported her through the difficult decision to leave her job and apply to a school of veterinary medicine. He'd stood by her when her father all but said she was no daughter of his. When Flynn found out that the school she wanted to go to was in Colorado, he'd suggested that they move there, confident that she would be accepted.

He believed in her more than she believed in herself.

"I love you, Flynn McCallister."

"I love you, too, but I'm still not going to let you do any of the packing. I'll do the china and we'll let the movers do the rest."

"Okay. But you're being overprotective."

"I like being overprotective."

She watched him move over to the box she'd been packing and start wrapping the china in tissue.

"Have you called your parents to tell them about the baby?"

"I talked to my mother. She was very excited."

"Did you talk to your dad?"

"Ann, forget it." His tone held a gentle warning. The subject of his father was off-limits. He said he'd accepted the rift between them, but she knew it still bothered him. Still, there was nothing she could do about it.

A knock at the door interrupted her thoughts. She started to get to her feet but Flynn waved her back. "Sit there and relax. It's probably the guy from the moving company. I told Joe to send him up when he got here."

Ann stood up as he walked to the door. It was nice that Flynn wanted to take care of her, but she wasn't going to act like Camille and greet visitors lying back on a sofa. She heard him open the door and then there was a long silence. Curiosity drew her forward.

Her eyes widened as Flynn stepped into the living room, his face absolutely expressionless. Behind him were his parents. Not just his mother, who had visited them on a number of occasions, but his father, too.

Ann came forward, holding out her hands. "Louise. How nice to see you." The two women hugged with real affection and then Ann was left facing her father-in-law. It was the first time she'd seen him in over a year. He hadn't even come to the small wedding. "Mr. McCallister. It's nice to see you." She held out her hand, not quite sure it was the right thing to do but needing to make some gesture.

He took her hand, his grip a little too tight, his eyes reflecting his uneasiness. "It's good to see you again, Ann. I . . . it would make me very happy if you would call me David. No need to be formal."

"Thank you, David." She looked at her husband, but Flynn was looking at one of the packing boxes. She could see the muscle that ticked in the side of his jaw and she knew how nervous he was. There'd be no help from him.

"Why don't you both come in and sit down. I think I've got some coffee in the kitchen and there's probably some banana bread left."

"That's all right, Ann. We had coffee before we left home." Louise followed her into the shambles of the living room, leaving the two men to trail behind, not speaking, looking anywhere but at each other.

The two women sat on the sofa and the men remained standing. Flynn leaned against the empty fireplace, his boneless slump making it clear that this visit meant nothing to him. His father stood next to the window, his blunt fingers shoved in the pockets of his suit coat.

Louise and Ann looked at each other and then looked at their respective husbands, letting the silence stretch. David met his wife's stern look and cleared his throat awkwardly.

"Your mother tells me that you and Ann are going to be having a child."

"Yes, we are."

"That's wonderful. Wonderful." David took his hands out of his pockets and stared at them for a moment as if not quite sure who they belonged to and then shoved them back into hiding.

"You're...ah...moving to Colorado, I understand."

"That's right." Flynn would have left it at that but he caught Ann's eyes, reading the plea in them. "Ann's going to be going to school there."

"Good. Good." The silence stretched again. "We...ah...that is, your mother and I thought we'd like to maybe help out with the...house. We...that is...I didn't get you a wedding present and it would mean a lot to us if you were to consider the house a wedding gift."

Ann held her breath, waiting for Flynn's answer. He had to see how difficult this was for his father. Surely, he wouldn't turn him away. Flynn glanced at her and then looked at his father.

"Thank you. Ann and I would be happy to accept your gift."

Ann let her breath out in a rush, feeling Louise do the same next to her. "Thank you, David. The house will mean even more to us, knowing that it comes from the two of you." David McCallister shifted uneasily beneath the warmth of her words.

"You know, Flynn, you've got a real treasure here. I hope you know how lucky you are. Marrying Ann is about the smartest thing you'll ever do. Just like marrying your mother was for me."

Flynn's face relaxed in a half smile. "You don't have to tell me how lucky I am. I know."

"Your mother tells me that you're quite a photographer. I never knew that. She says you've even submitted some things to a few magazines."

"That was Ann's doing. She can be pretty stubborn." His smile was so loving that Ann had to swallow the lump in her throat.

"Well, good luck with them. I'm . . . I'm proud of you, son."

Flynn's eyes widened as he stared at his father. "Thank you . . ." The two men stared at each other across the years, across a lot of hurts. The distance couldn't be wiped out in one short visit, but the first steps had been taken. "It means a lot to me to hear you say that."

Ann sniffed, unashamed of the tears that filled her eyes. David looked at his son for a moment and then looked away.

"Well, we can't stay long. You've got a lot to get done."

Ann didn't urge them to stay longer. Perhaps it was best to keep this first visit short. At the door, she hugged Louise tightly and then hesitated a moment before tentatively putting her arms around her father-in-law's stocky figure. He patted her on the back, the gesture awkward, as if it had been too long since he'd shown anyone any softness.

Flynn hugged his mother and then faced his father. After a moment, David held out his hand and Flynn took it. More was said in the fervency of their grips than could have been said with words.

"Keep in touch, Flynn. Losing one son in a lifetime is enough for any man." He was gone before Flynn could reply, the door closing quietly behind him and his wife.

Flynn stared at the door for a moment and then turned to see Ann watching him, tears running down her face. His own eyes were suspiciously bright.

He held out his arms and she stepped into them, linking her arms around his waist, pressing her face to his chest. She could feel the strong beat of his heart beneath her cheek. It felt so right.

"I love you so much." His voice broke on the words and he buried his face in her hair.

Her arms tightened around his waist. As long as she had him to hold on to, everything in her life was right.

PAMELA BROWNING

...is fireworks on the green at the Fourth of July and prayers said around the Thanksgiving table. It is the dream of freedom realized in thousands of small towns across this great nation.

But mostly, the Heartland is its people. People who care about and help one another. People who cherish traditional values and give to their children the greatest gift, the gift of love.

American Romance presents HEARTLAND, an emotional trilogy about people whose memories, hopes and dreams are bound up in the acres they farm.

HEARTLAND...the story of America.

Don't miss these heartfelt stories: American Romance #237 SIMPLE GIFTS (March), #241 FLY AWAY (April), and #245 HARVEST HOME (May).

HRT-1

MAIL-IN-OFFER
------ OFFER CERTIFICATE ------

I have enclosed the required number of proofs of purchase from any specially marked "Gifts From The Heart" Harlequin romance book, plus cash register receipts and a check or money order payable to Harlequin Gifts From The Heart Offer, to cover postage and handling.

002

CHECK ONE	ITEM	# OF PROOFS OF PURCHASE	POSTAGE & HANDLING FEE
	01 Brass Picture Frame	2	$ 1.00
	02 Heart-Shaped Candle Holders with Candles	3	$ 1.00
	03 Heart-Shaped Keepsake Box	4	$ 1.00
	04 Gold-Plated Heart Pendant	5	$ 1.00
	05 Collectors' Doll Limited quantities available	12	$ 2.75

NAME _____

STREET ADDRESS _____ APT. # _____

CITY _____ STATE _____ ZIP _____

Mail this certificate, designated number of proofs of purchase (inside back page) and check or money order for postage and handling to:

Gifts From The Heart, P.O. Box 4814
Reidsville, N. Carolina 27322-4814

NOTE THIS IMPORTANT OFFER'S TERMS

Requests must be postmarked by May 31, 1988. Only proofs of purchase from specially marked "Gifts From The Heart" Harlequin books will be accepted. This certificate plus cash register receipts and a check or money order to cover postage and handling must accompany your request and may not be reproduced in any manner. Offer void where prohibited, taxed or restricted by law. LIMIT ONE REQUEST PER NAME, FAMILY, GROUP, ORGANIZATION OR ADDRESS. Please allow up to 8 weeks after receipt of order for shipment. Offer only good in the U.S.A. Hurry—Limited quantities of collectors' doll available. Collectors' dolls will be mailed to first 15,000 qualifying submitters. All other submitters will receive 12 free previously unpublished Harlequin books and a postage & handling refund.

OFFER-1RR

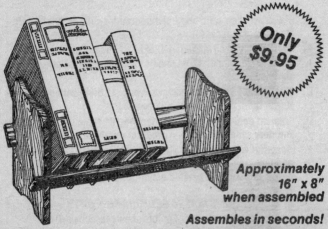

GIFTS FROM THE HEART
from *Harlequin*

FREE BY MAIL With proofs of purchase plus postage and handling

A. Hand-polished solid brass picture frame 1-5/8″ × 1-3/8″ with 2 proofs of purchase.

B. Individually handworked, pair of heart-shaped glass candle holders (2″ diameter), 6″ candles included, with 3 proofs of purchase.

C. Heart-shaped porcelain keepsake box (1″ high) with delicate flower motif with 4 proofs of purchase.

D. Radiant gold-plated heart pendant on 16″ chain with complimentary satin pouch with 5 proofs of purchase.

E. Beautiful collectors' doll with genuine porcelain face, hands and feet, and a charming heart appliqué on dress with 12 proofs of purchase. Limited quantities available. See offer terms.

HERE IS HOW TO GET YOUR FREE GIFTS

Send us the required number of proofs of purchase (below) of specially marked "Gifts From The Heart" Harlequin books and cash register receipts with the Offer Certificate (available in the back pages) properly completed, plus a check or money order (do not send cash) payable to Harlequin Gifts From The Heart Offer. We'll RUSH you your specified gift. Hurry—Limited quantities of collectors' doll available. See offer terms.

401R

GIFTS FROM THE HEART
ONE PROOF
OF PURCHASE

To collect your free gift by mail you must include the necessary number of proofs of purchase with order certificate.